Nelson Nye

TRAIL OF
LOST SKULLS

G.K. HALL &CO.
Boston, Massachusetts
1991

Published in Large Print by arrangement with
Nelson Nye.

G.K. Hall Large Print Book Series.

Set in 16 pt. Plantin.

Library of Congress Cataloging-in-Publication Data

Nye, Nelson C. (Nelson Coral), 1907–
    Trail of lost skulls / Nelson Nye.
      p.   cm. — (G.K. Hall large print book series) (Nightingale
series)
   ISBN 0-8161-4832-5
   1. Large type books. I. Title.
  [PS3527.Y33T736   1991]
  813'.54—dc20   91-4111

For
DON WOLLHEIM

THE SUN was dropping red as a pomegranate behind a murk of smelter smoke when Yavapai Jones, topping out on a ridge, scowled down with a bitter twist of the lips on the booming copper camp of Redskin. It lay spilled across the bottom of the canyon like the vicious excrescence from a ruptured boil; corrugated iron, belching stacks, a maze of gallowsframes and tarpaper shanties puking out of the hillsides like hell wouldn't have them, yet rich beyond the dreams of Midas, and Yavapai heaved a disgruntled sigh. The claims he filed hadn't turned out like this and his soul was crammed with a sour disgust.

Cursing, snarling, he went through his pockets for the price of a drink but all he got up for this outlay of effort was a solitary pair of discolored pennies.

He flung them away with a grumbling oath. It was hard lines for sure when a man of his talents who had been all over was reduced to shooting the breeze for a whistle! Cowpuncher, freighter—a guy more cunning than the wiliest Apache, he'd been around long enough to be sure whatever was told of this trip had got to top anything told before if he was minded to continue on public funds.

It wasn't so much the drinks he had cadged as the streak of hard luck he couldn't seem to get shucked of. Give a dog a bad name and he'd two strikes against him— he'd seen them spit when his back was turned! He could add three and two! There was a hereafter coming for some of these sports and he hoped to be there when the croppers caught up with them.

Man would think, by grab, he had smallpox or something!

Muttering, grimacing, feeling hard used as Job, Jones yanked off his salt-rimed sun-puckered hat to haul one dust-crusted sleeve across the face he had shaved three days ago in anticipation of a visit he couldn't put off any longer. He had never been one to pamper his stomach but an unrelieved diet of lizard tails and hoppers mighty sure left a man standing twice to cast a shadow.

He peered again down below with a look of repugnance. A scatter of lights now picked out the camp and a heady aroma of supper fires curling out of the canyon pretty near turned him dizzy. It fetched a bray from his burro and Jones laid hold of the rope just in time.

"Hee-haw yourself, you dad-dratted jackass!" he croaked through cracked lips, and brought the animal into sullen submission. "We'll go when I say so—not a dang minute sooner!"

It was only putting off the inevitable, but now that he had the camp firmly in sight Yavapai felt an increasing reluctance to confronting himself with its penny-pinching denizens. Stretching the truth didn't warp his system, but a man had his pride. He hadn't the ghost of a hope of talking up another grubstake. But where else could he try with nothing but one gimpy burro to lean on?

Redskin was the jumping-off place, end of the line any way you cut it. Nothing beyond but sand, heat, and Injuns which would liefer lift hair than any other thing a body could konjer—particular now with this busted treaty and the hate worked up over that buffalo slaughter.

Feeling hollowed out and perky as a .22 cartridge in a ten gauge gun, Jones with halter shank round his rump set off stiff-legged down the boulder-strewn slope to what any kid in three-cornered pants could have guessed wouldn't be no hero's welcome. If he got no worse than sneers and opprobrium he could count himself lucky. Some guys had been known to leave this camp forking a rail in a coat of feathers!

It was hardly a prospect to firm up the red corpuscles. When a man backs a loser with his own cash money he isn't of a mind to be choosy of words and Jones had already walked off with three backers' hopes. He could have made out to stand up to that, he thought, if only his last patron hadn't been a woman. Hi gollies, he must have been out of his mind, he told himself, trying to stiffle a shudder.

She was smoking a cigar when one of her croupiers knocked on the door of her upstairs hideaway with word that Jones had just been sighted.

"How do his packs look, Fetterman?"

"Ain't got no packs."

The cigar traveled over leathery lips. "What," she gruffly called back, "has he got?" huffing smoke through the words like a Saint George dragon.

"One limpin' burro. That's about the size of it."

The big rawboned creature with the outlandish pompadour overhanging the raddled fiercely crimsoned cheeks put down her knitting and crushed out her cigar. Regrets never buttered no parsnips. She might secretly admire a man's talking talents and the bare-faced gall of his preposterous claims but she had, after all, a reputation to sustain.

"All right. I'll take care of this." Big Ass Liz got up out of her rocker. "Keep him busy till I git into my corsets."

Jones was in no hurry to reach his set-to with Liz. There was left but one place in this brawling camp where he could look for condolence or reasonably expect any semblance of the welcome due a man of his exploits. That haven was the Starbuck Cafe and, as he hitched his burro to the peeled pole out front, his stare crossed a shoulder in a furtive glance at the louvered doors of the Sparrow-hawk Bar.

So far, so good. He was not so naïve as to imagine Liz would not know of this arrival. Hustling into the hash house he was sweatily thankful the mascaraed harridan wasn't halfway here with a gun in each fist. He had no doubt but what she soon enough would be. Time enough, however, to cross burned bridges when a man couldn't find any other way around.

Ignoring the following stares of two miners holding down stools at the oilcloth covered counter, Jones tramped on through a curtained arch into the heat and smells of the cubbyhole kitchen. "Where's Hes?" he hailed the aproned proprietor crouched red-faced above the hot stove.

Pop Leddabrand, slanching a dubious scowl, wiped the drip off his nose and declared without warmth, "Expect she'll be back afore you take off again."

Jones looked him over. "When we get hitched," he pronounced with a sniff, "first thing I'll do is put you to pasture."

Pop had heard that wind blow before. "When you get hitched the ice across hell will be hard enough t' hold up an iron horse! Why don't you stay away from her, Jones?"

"You wanta see her growed into a dried-up old maid?"

"It's what I keep tellin' her. There's no future with you."

"She knows better'n that." If Jones was offended he kept it hid. The aquiline nose above the curled-up ends of his red moustache remained as complacent as the hoot of a rooster; the eyes remained blue pools of assurance; twin oases nested in the sun wrinkles around them. Worst of all, he grinned. In Pop's experience that white-toothed grin was the hatefullest thing about him. It was what the women couldn't ever get enough of.

"I've had a run of hard luck," Yavapai offered. "Whatever become of that pipsqueak carpet drummer—"

"She's out with him now. They went ridin'," Pop said, turning back to his flapjacks.

"Couldn't be in better hands." Yavapai beamed as if this arrangement had his completest approval. "Time she gets through totin' him home the company of a real up-and'-comer like me me will look more blessed than the pearly gates."

Airing his teeth in a satisfied smirk he helped himself from a jar filled with doughnuts, cramming his mouth as he headed for the front. Just before he reached the curtain, however, a bell began to jangle on the opened front door. "Where is he?" Fetterman's voice filled the room. "Of all the slippery two-legged no-accounts that ever took advantage of a trusting woman—"

Jones, putting down the uneaten frag-

7

ment of a preempted goody, gave a tug to his belt and shoved through the curtain. "You vociferatin' about me?"

"You know it," Fetterman said without preamble. "Considering how much she's invested in your travels—"

"If you're referrin' to my partner, the philanthropic Liz, I'll thank you to use a kindlier tone," Jones said, huffing up like a prodded toad. "What she bought was not me, just a share in one venture, and I've got to admit it turned out pretty rocky. But the worm always turns, my good fellow. If your principle cares to make a further investment I'll be happy to attend her at my earliest—"

"Never mind the fifty-cent tour," Fetterman sneered. "If you want to stay healthy you'll get over there, pronto!"

Jones pulled himself to full height, eyes glittery. "You didn't traipse over here to threaten me, did you?"

Confronted with this belligerence Fetterman shrugged. "You know Liz. You want her really on the prod keep perambulatin' round."

"Apology accepted," Yavapai grumbled, peeling the killer look off his face. The whole camp knew what kind of tantrums Liz could throw and—being a woman—get away with it; but a man had a kind of obligation to himself. With this pair of Cousin Jacks lapping it up—not to mention old Pop banging pots in the kitchen, he had to take a high hand. He peered down his nose. "Tell her soon's I can find the time I'll be over."

"Wouldn't wait too long if I was you," Fetterman grinned.

While Jones was dejectedly finishing his supper—on the cuff, as usual—expecting momentarily to have Liz descend on him, Hester Leddabrand returned from her outing with the carpet man, smiling timidly at Jones when she found him at the counter.

While no prize, certainly, she was the best that was available. Chief drone and biscuit shooter, of somewhat better than medium height, she had hazel eyes under a muss of mousy hair, a pretty fair set of ankles and prospects of taking over the business when her old man wore himself out of the boss job. While there'd been no firm bid either passed or accepted, it was generally assumed throughout the camp that if Jones ever made up his mind to get hitched she would be his number one choice for helpmeet.

9

Possibly this was at the bottom of the flustery look she popped in his direction as the salesman of carpets limped in on her heels.

It was Hester's misfortune to feel all thumbs whenever she was near him, for Jones, while hardly in a class with Fremont or Bridger, was after all—let's face it—a kind of legend at this end of the cactus.

Needless to say she did not share the general estimate. Tremendously admiring yet nervously unable to gauge his interest in her or even vaguely to grasp a scanty quarter of his embroideries, she lived for his smile and was, in consequence, more than just a little upset at having him discover her in the company of another.

But with the bell still jangling, and before she could speak, the play was abruptly taken out of her hands. A spindly little white collar type she had not seen before and hence obviously a stranger, rudely elbowing the drummer aside, stepped into the picture like a bolt from the blue.

A brown derby hat was cockily perched on his head; the coat pockets of his store suit bulged with folded papers and a city cigarette that noticeably wabbled when he spoke clung precariously from the bulge of an outthrust lower lip. "I'm looking for Ya-vapai Jones," he declaimed, and in the shocked silence that fell at these words Jones was suddenly the target of every turned eye in the place.

Peering down his long nose, Liz's uneasy partner, unhappily wondering if he was about to be roped by some kind of process server sent out by his enemies up at the county seat, hardly knew whether he'd best deny his identity or coolly admit and hope to brazen it out. There was always the chance they might have him dead to rights; but ere he could decide which way to jump, Hester, unaware of his problems, in her most helpful tone put the finger on him. "That is Mr. Jones—the gentleman with the snakeskin band on his hat."

II

To be stabbed in the back by his nearest and dearest is the kind of experience shouldn't happen to a dog. The expression stark in Jones' startled stare must have greatly resembled the look *You Too* Brutus probably got from Caesar.

With his lips ground together, Hester,

stricken, clapped both hands across her big mouth, but the damage was done. The stranger's glance pushed and probed like a horse trader out to fetch down the price.

"Well," Jones said, facing up to it, "what's on your mind besides that stiff hat?"

"Name's Harragan—Bill Harragan," Stiff Hat said like it was running neck and neck with names like Grant and John Wilkes Booth, adding testily when it got no change out of Yavapai, "leg man for the Boston Transcript." When that got nothing out of Jones either, he said with a sour kind of bile in his tone: "You the one been hoorawin' these widders and orphans? Sellin' 'em shares in mines never found?"

That appeared to hit Jones between wind and water to judge by the sinking look coming out of him. But he'd been through sticky wickets before, a clear strain fighter who never said die till the last round was fired. Kind of shaking himself he got the chin off his chest. "Goin' to let you in on something, mister. You taken a look at our local Boot Hill?"

When Harragan stared, Jones said soft as spider's feet, "It's one of them places folks don't come back from," and set a big hand against the butt of his six-shooter.

The journalist's expression did not reveal any panic flash but the sound of his chuckle wasn't awfully contagious. The whole room listened while it plowed through the silence. It was plain he would get no help from these yokels. They might not care two hoots for Jones but as compared to strangers they stood solidly behind him.

"Guess you're the feller," Harragan grimaced, trying out another hook. "Gentleman over at the Knife & Arrow appears some anxious to have a word with you."

Jones, passing a hand across his scraggle of beard, cocked a jaundiced eye. "He sent you after me?"

"Nobody sends Bill Harragan anywheres."

That wasn't going to buy him anything either. A soft answer, he was reminded, sometimes turns away wrath. "Look—" he said, putting a little wheedle into it. "I'm tryin' to do the both of you a favor."

But Jones had met Greeks bearing gifts before. He swung around on his stool and went back to his groceries.

Harragan's cheeks took on a tarnished glow. But, controlling himself, he said to

Jones' back: "You don't understand—why you think my rag's sending me round with this feller? Because he's Big News, man. In the world of fossils C. Culpepper Cutteridge rates the front page! Be to your advantage to spare him a few moments."

But Jones went right on feeding his tape-worm.

Harragan, glaring, did a slow burn. There had to be someway a feller . . . Suddenly inspired, the *Transcript's* man tipped back his derby to declare with unction, "It was Miles himself put Cutteridge onto you—Nelson A. Miles, the Big Chief in person—heard 'im myself. Claimed you was just what the doctor ordered. Said if anyone could do it—"

Harragan, jaw dropping, jumped back in alarm. Like a butt-shot grizzly Jones was off his stool with his stare winnowed down to glittering slits. "You got any more bull tucked up your sleeve?"

"Cripes, as God is my witness—"

"Save your breath. Miles wouldn't throw me a rope if I was drowndin'. That old hypothecator sat up nights tryin' to figure out ways he could get himself shut of me!"

Harragan said warily, "I can't help that. Way he put it to Cutty, you could track a damn fly straight across bare rock. Said if anyone could help him you was the guy."

"How much you gettin' outa this?" Jones snorted. Yet in spite of himself he was beginning to show interest. "What's this Cutteridge want me to do?"

"Shh—" Harragan cautioned, snatching his glance from a grime-fogged window, "here he comes now! He can tell you himself."

The bell on the yanked-open door bawled again. The man who stepped in could hardly have been more than five foot three in button-top shoes two shades lighter than mustard. It appeared obvious he was either a dude or a Britisher, neither of which Jones could scarcely abide.

He was got up in a store suit of coarse-woven tweed sporting baggy-kneed trousers and bulged coat pockets. On his head was the sorriest excuse for a hat Jones in his travels had yet encountered. Cloth it was and flat as a stove lid. A Tartan plaid with a long green bill and a button on top to maybe hang the thing up by.

Except for the face Jones might have laughed, but here in the flesh was the spitting image of Ebenezer Scrooge, a militant killjoy with mutton-chop whiskers growing down to the jowls about a prissy mouth that was tight with impatience. Flinty eyes skewered Harragan like a long-beaked bird going after a worm. "Do you realize what time it is getting to be?"

"Sorry about that, but I found him," the reporter said with a flick of the hand that suggested a magician about to deliver his shiniest production. "Meet Yavapai Jones!" His grin rang out like a flutter of trumpets. "Jones, shake hands with Professor Cutteridge."

The great man, staring, put out a hand, but Jones didn't notice. All his attention was hypnotically focused on that still-open door where a young girl stood like a startled fawn. Such a breathtaking vision never before had come his way—not even in his horniest dreams; he was about as wrapped up as a hashish smoker with his first glimpse of paradise, jaw hanging down like a blacksmith's apron, when Harragan nudged him. "Wake up!" he growled and then, all smiles: "Shake hands with Professor Cutteridge, the man who discovered the three-toed horse."

Still in a trance Jones found the extended hand and pumped it, but his eyes stayed fixed on the girl in the door.

"I've got to talk with you, Jones," the man of science began, and Yavapai nodded. "No doubt about it," he said in a mumble. "Cute as a bug's ear an' twice as delightful!"

Cutteridge, blinking, peered around and, adding up what he could see, gruffly announced, "My daughter, Francie," as though he would like to get down to business.

Business was the farthest thing from Jones' mind. By all the signs and signal-smokes, he appeared about as mixed up as Hester had seen him, gulping through the silly smile on his face, wiping one paw along the leg of his Levi's, peering surprised life from it to Miss Cutteridge and, red-cheeked, blurting: "Powerful pleased, ma'am—*powerful!*"

Miss Cutteridge, eying him doubtfully, came timidly nearer and then, brightly radiant, took that rock-scarred fist in both her own. "The General has told us so much about you," she said with her eyes beaming into his face; "it is almost like you're one of the family."

Hester's father, coming out of the kitchen, stood wiping his hands on a grease-spattered apron, taking this in with obvious relish. It was somewhat harder to read Hester's look though her stiffened cheeks rather gave the impression there might be a storm building up in the offing.

"Just wait till I write the girls back home," Francie tinkled, clamped tight to her trophy. "They'll be green with envy when they learn I'm out in this gorgeous country holding hands with—Harragan! You've got a camera. Do take our picture!"

Cutteridge gruffly cleared his throat. "Time enough for that after I've had my talk with him. Mister Jones," he said, "we'd esteem it a privilege to have you for dinner. May we count on it, sir?"

"Well . . ." Jones drawled, looking dubiously around him, "as a matter of—"

"Nothing formal, of course" the professor assured him. "Just a leisurely meal to sort of further our acquaintance. Guess you know where we are—room 206 at the top of the stairs. We eat promptly at seven."

Jones seemed to go a little pale around the gills when his glance encountered Hester, but Francie didn't give him any chance to back out. "Of course he'll come!!" she told her father brightly, and what could he do after that but agree?

18

III

WHEN THE Cutteridges—father, Francie and their bird dog reporter—departed the smells of the Leddabrand gastronomical parlor, Yavapai, prodded by a sudden uneasiness, attempted to up-anchor and sail in their wake. Which was pretty shrewd thinking, though somewhat belated.

Before he could slip through the banged-shut door, the daughter of the house, through the strident clangor of its still-jangling bell, sank an authoritative grip on the back of his beltstrap and dug in her heels like the horse of a roper.

"Just a minute!" she purred through white rimmed lips. "Can't you think of any matters we had better get straight before you go panting after that strumpet?"

Yavapai stopped like he'd run into a wall. Without quite being aware of the fact, he'd been afraid all along that, despite all his precautions, he might one of these days run into some frail who would not be compatible to folding her tent with aplomb and good taste when the dictates of spring directed him elsewhere.

But who could have dreamed it would be mousy Hess, the hash house keeper's daughter with her rabbit's timidity and eyes big as saucepans? Such perfidy staggered him. He felt reduced inside to a quivering jelly and had to summon all his starch to keep from seeming like a ninny.

There are occasions when it's wiser to cut one's losses than attempt to cope with the buffetings of fate, and Jones was not slow to reach a conclusion. Better to put the show on the road. But one look at that jaw—clenched now like a cudgel below the green glare—confirmed the worst of his fears and told all too plain she would not be put off by any white lies.

She was girding herself to make a scene you could date time by. Yet worse—much worse—was the look in Pop's eye as, reaching through the curtain, he brought forth his big bore double-barreled Greener. "Stay put!" he told the squirming Yavapai. "Nobody runs out on *my* daughter, dang you!"

Seemed like things were about as bad as they were likely to get when Big Ass Liz flung open the door. Jones tried to call up a righteous wrath but all that came out was a piteous groan. It wasn't only Liz who came marching in. Right behind her was Harragan, face stretched in a grin, nose on a story, armed with notebook and pencil.

With the paint scrubbed into those eroded cheeks and that ginger mop piled atop her head like a portable sunset that swirled and dipped with every twitch of her bosoms, Liz wasted no time getting down to brass tacks. "Just answer me plain. Did you or did you not accept a grubstake from me?"

Since their agreement was a matter of public record with the stake attested to by his John Henry there wasn't much point in Yavapai denying it. So all he said was, "Yes, ma'am," meekly, and hoped she wasn't about to climb on her high horse with that butter-faced Harragan gawking and smirking while he waited for details to send to his paper.

Liz pinned him with a half-shut eye. "And what were the terms of that agreement?"

On stronger ground Jones said with a chuckle, "Why get in a sweat when I didn't find anything?"

"You'll find out about sweat before I get done. That paper was dated to run six months and there's still thirty days before it expires. If you imagined my intention was to support you in idleness you can disabuse yourself of that notion right now. Sorry," she said in an aside to Hester, "but I've got a prior claim on this cantankerous lout." And, to Jones: "Git into your hat an' head for the Sparrowhawk!"

The grin ran off Jones' face like water. "But—but—"

"Don't you 'but' me! You hike over there, pronto. When I got time comin' I aim to git it. An' I'm seizin' that burro and any other possibles—"

"But I can't go *now!*"

"This gun says different," Liz cut him off, shaking out of her sleeve a short-barreled pocket pistol. "I'd sure hate to puncture your everlastin' envelope, but don't push too hard. I might forgit I'm a Christian."

So off they went, Jones bitterly fuming; Liz, with a wintry smile on her teeth, holding the pistol at his bristling back. Fetterman, propping up an outside corner, gave a jerk on the halter shank and putting his shoulder to it, brought up the rear with Jones' confiscated burro.

In their make-do suite at the Knife & Arrow with the dinner all laid and Francie dressed and perfumed to the nines, Cutteridge, abruptly halting his stride and not for the first time fetching out his hunting case, squinting irascibly, told his daughter, "We'll not wait any longer!"

"But, Daddy, he said—"

"I don't care what he said!" the discoverer of the three-toed horse snapped angrily. "When a man's word isn't to be relied upon, Francie, there is little about him to merit further interest."

Without more ado he drew up his chair, leaving his daughter to do likewise or stand there. It was plain in this mood he didn't care which. But Francie, wringing her hands, tried again to postpone the meal's commencement. "You know General Miles—"

"I'll admit Miles appeared to be convinced of his ability," her father said, helping himself to the main course. "But the ability to keep one's word, it seems to me, is of far more importance than the unstable tolerance of a few bare-ass Indians. I imagine we shall find other scouts who can—"

"But with Yavapai's acknowledged distinctions? His elan? Experience? His standing with these savages? I think we had better be practical, Daddy. You know, they call him 'Broken Hat.' The General told me that's a mark of respect for his prowess as a fighter and other abilities they hold in esteem. Besides," she said firmly, "who else knows the Bridger Basin as he does?"

Cutteridge pulled at his lip, undecided. "He probably knows his geography and he *might* be the slickest scout ever employed by the Army but that doesn't excuse his personal habits. Miles gave me a look at the other side of him and I can tell you it's a pretty ugly picture. The fellow's shiftless, improvident, a boozer and womanizer— some of the things I was told would turn your stomach. They finally had to get rid of him."

"Why?"

"Because the fellow's insubordinate. When he didn't like an order he ignored it completely!"

Francie did not appear to count that so terrible. "Perhaps," she said thoughtfully, "you would have, too, had you been in his place. The Army can come up with some pretty wild notions, and some of these 'gentlemen' fresh from the Point—"

"I'll remind you that Miles is an experienced officer."

"Perhaps all his staff haven't had his advantages," Francie pointed out with a remembering smile. "Some of those shavetails can be pretty impetuous . . ." She broke off, turning, as a heavy tread climbed the hall stairs outside. The door shook to a set of peremptory knuckles and Harragan, on a word from her father, came in with a grin vastly stretching his countenance.

Cutteridge stared testily. "I could do with a good laugh myself about now. What do you find in this godforsaken place—"

"You'll never believe it, but that feller Jones you came over here to hire—Do you know where he is?"

"He's *supposed* to be here. I invited him to dinner."

"Well, he's not going to come," declared the professor's correspondent to the Boston *Transcript*, half drowning the words in the gust of his laughter. "They've got him to mopping floors at the Sparrowhawk."

"Mopping floors!" Francie cried. "You're not serious, surely?"

"Go look for yourself—just follow the crowd. He's swamping all right," Harragan said with a chuckle. "The she hippopotamus that runs that dive—name of Liz, I believe—is the dame that staked him to this last prowl for plunder. He returned emptyhanded with a month still to go and this character—Liz—allows she's going to work it out of his hide. Ho-ho! Yep, he's sweating like a galley slave. She hauled him out of the Buckhorn at gunpoint."

Francie and her father exchanged shocked glances.

Harragan, wiping his eyes, still sniggered. "The hero of Cotterpin!" he gagged with a bellyshake. "I could have told you the guy was considerably overrated, but to come down to this . . . Still," he said, sobering, "it might work out better. Way things stand now he hasn't much choice. If you're bound and determined to have him, Cutty, all you got to do is bail the poor slob out."

Cutteridge slanched him a rather wry look. But encroachments of familiarity he could manage to abide—even a diminutive obnoxious as 'Cutty,' so long as this bounder kept his back-East readers happily entranced with Cutteridge claims to international celebrity.

In a world gone mad with the search for missing links which might conclusively hitch man to an ancestry of apes a paleontologist who couldn't unearth one had need of all the kudos his brains could put his hands on.

Silent, he chewed his lip in scowling thought.

"From what I've heard about these grub-stakes," Harragan urged, "it wouldn't take much—no more'n a evening at one of your clubs. It's not like you had to watch every penny now you've come into your uncle's inheritance. Why," he said with a leer, "you could buy half this territory and give it back—"

"When I need financial advise, Mister Harragan, I'll keep the benefits of your experience where they properly belong."

"I was just trying to help—"

"Sometimes a man would rather make his own blunders. Please close the door on your way down the stairs."

Harragan, flushing, took his departure.

"It's the obvious answer," Francie said.

Cutteridge scowled. "I suppose so." However well conceived, he was not one to take any great amount of pleasure in coups stumbled onto by somebody else. "I am not at all sure this fellow Jones will work out." But, pushing back from the table, he scooped up his hat. "The people one has to work with these days . . ." He let out a long sigh. "I think, my dear, you had better stay here."

Francie regarded him with troubled eyes. "Do try to hang onto your temper, Daddy. Some of these specimens seem a little sub-human."

IV

CUTTERIDGE DID not squander much thought on the alarms of his daughter or the charybdis of his own testy temper. It was woman's nature to be burdened with worries, to invest in a thousand unfounded fears. He felt perfectly capable of looking after himself. How did she suppose he had managed to get by for the seventeen years it had taken her to grow up?

Tramping the unregarded short quarter-mile between his hotel and the locale of Jones' enforced labors it was no concern for himself which drew the professor's mind away from its engrossment with the perplexities of a world much nearer his heart. It wasn't really premonition, a more a vague disquiet occasioned by the reminder of his conversation with Miles.

The general had stoutly talked up the

many sterling qualities of his ex-scout; it was only when Harragan with his newsman's curiosity had bluntly asked why Jones wasn't still a part of the frontier complex that the general, obviously trying to cover an embarrassment, reluctantly admitted to having terminated his services.

Pressed, he had acknowledged the man's insubordination, his refusal to follow orders which went against his grain. Under Harragan's hobnailed pursuit of the topic other foibles had emerged, the periodic benders, his involvement with women and the careless disregard with which he spent his wages.

Cutteridge's puritanical concepts, harking back to that talk, could scarcely repress a shudder. The sole example given concerned a Saturday night when the scout—his pockets stuffed with pay—had squandered the lot on a place of ill repute, hiring the establishment to close its doors while—like a raja among scented cushions—he had sat with a jug, naked as a jaybird, watching the soiled doves gambol and frolic till the M.P.'s had dumped him, sodden, in the guardhouse.

Yet, distasteful as this sordid episode was, it was the man's refusal to follow orders

29

which was at the seat of Cutteridge's dis-turbance. If there'd been anyone else with half Jones's knowledge the professor would not have stirred from his suit. But whom could he find so ideally fitted for the job in hand?

Still tugged two ways Cutteridge sur-veyed the saloon and finally, prim lips set in an expression of displeasure, reluctantly stepped through its half-leaf doors into a dimness that stank of evils too wicked to contemplate.

When his eyes adjusted to the change in light he was able to make out a dark bar along one side; a loose arrangement of tables occupying the other. Four men in rough dress leaned against the bar; a white father figure with folded arms stood back of it. Girls sat with men at some of the tables and the paleontologist's first startled glance con-firmed everything he'd been told about such devil-spawned dens of iniquity.

Hastily, averting his fascinated stare he marched, self-conscious and flushed of cheek, to a place at the bar not contaminated by custom and said to the apron when that worthy strolled over, "I've been given to understand a man named Jones is employed at this place."

The barkeep's poker look catalogued the outlandish getup, drifted back to Cutteridge's face without batting an eye. Leaning carefully forward, he put his mouth beside the handiest ear and said in the sepulchral tones of a conspirator: "That's him off yonder diggin' out them spittoons."

Cutteridge shuddered. After some hesitation he said like he'd gone a long while without water, "Kindly inform the proprietress I'd like a few words on a matter of mutual interest—and profit," he added when the apron didn't move. "The name is Cutteridge."

"That supposed to mean somethin'?"

The professor fixed him with a fish-belly stare. "Just tell her," he said, obviously not minded to scatter pearls before swine.

The barkeep shrugged, caught the eye of a house man and went back to his customers. The frockcoated gambler, forsaking a promising layout of solitaire, got grudgingly up and with a hard look at Cutteridge, went off with clamped lips through a bead-draped doorway.

Cutteridge, morosely studying his fingernails, was having second thoughts about the entire matter when a whisky roughened voice said from five feet away: "You lookin' for me?"

In all his studies both at home and abroad never had Cutteridge's jerked-open eyes beheld the like of the vertebrate before him. Some pretty weird specimens he had certainly seen but this ginger haired harpy with the painted cheeks had him back on his heels completely stripped of words.

"Come, come!" she said, clearing her throat with impatience. "I believe you mentioned a matter of profit?"

"Mmm—yes!" Cutteridge gulped, backing off against the bar. "I . . . ah—"

"You don't have to mince words with me," Liz growled. She paid no heed to the titters this fetched, but when his eyes jerked around as though seeking a bolt hole she said, misinterpreting the cause of his fluster, "If it's bein' overheard you're so squeamish about we can go upstairs—"

He cried aghast: "No, no—you don't understand. It's about this fellow Jones."

"Yavapai?" She peered at him sharply. "You cuttin' a rusty?"

When he stood there the picture of baffled confusion, Liz yelled: "Jones! Step over here."

They both watched him straighten, wipe

his hands on his pantlegs. The whole place watched, patently enjoying this, particularly the spectacle of that damnfool earl with his popped-open mouth and muttonchop whiskers, his cheeks fired up like Aurora Borealis. It wasn't often they found a Britisher at such disadvantage.

Cutteridge, of course, had no idea what they were thinking. He fervently wished he hadn't come here. Then Jones, with a hangdog grin, shuffled over. The hennaed caricature of a two-legged woman rasped: "Know this jasper?"

Jones and the outlander swapped bristly glances. "Never saw him before!" Jones vehemently declared, determined to be innocent until proven otherwise.

The professor looked startled.

Jones, knuckling an eye, hitched up his jeans, and—when Liz failed to call off his punishment—appeared on the verge of reluctantly returning to his scrub brush and cuspidors.

"Just a moment, my good fellow," Cutteridge gruffed in the tone of Moses handing down the twelve tablets. He brought his look around to Liz. "I am about to make a trek into the wilderness—"

"Then you ought to be bored for the simples," Liz growled. "If you don't care a whoop for your own hair, mister, you could have some regard for the rest of us settlers. All them red devils need is a mite of encouragement."

"I assume you're referring to the Indian unrest? I have just been with Miles. If we are able to come to some equitable arrangement I'm prepared to offer Jones a stipend as guide."

"You an' him again' the whole Choctaw Nation?"

"I shall make it worth his while. As a matter of fact there'll be others in the party—"

Liz threw up her hands. "If he's fool enough to do it *I* won't stand in his way. But, as of right now, he's got a debt to work out. If you're still of a mind to commit suicide, drop by next month and—"

"I'm afraid that won't do. It won't do at all. We plan to set out first thing in the morning. If we're to have his services the matter will have to be settled right now."

A speculative gleam came into Liz's stare. "Just what did you have in mind?"

Cutteridge was no fool. "To what extent is Jones in your debt?"

"Well now, that'll take a mite of figgerin'.

34

There's the matter of them thirty days I've got coming. The two burros that turned up missing—pick, shovel, miscellaneous supplies. . . ."

Breaking in impatiently, Cutteridge gruffed: "Put a price on it, Madam."

Jones plaintively inquired, "Don't I git to say—"

"You'll do as you're told if you know what's good fer you," Liz cut him off. She peered at Cutteridge again. "What would you say to five hundred dollars?"

"I wasn't planning to pay heart balm," the professor said dryly.

"Would you go to three hundred?"

Cutteridge appeared to turn it over in his mind. "Tell you what," he said abruptly. "In view of the hazards and your financial involvement, why don't we work out a sort of lend-lease?"

"What's that?"

"Nothin' doing," Jones said. "I'm free, white an' twenty-one. She ain't lendin' me to anybody—"

"Be quiet!" Liz snapped. "Better still, go clean them drains." She flashed her three gold teeth. "You was sayin', mister?"

"I'll pay the three hundred as a kind of proviso. When I fetch him back, sound of limb and available, you return half of it. If we don't come back you keep the whole thing."

Liz actually beamed. "Now you're talkin'," she said, and stuck out her hand.

V

JONES, WHEN he heard of the arrangement, crow hopped around like a sore-footed mule. "I'm no goddam *peon!*" he snarled. "What the hell are you tryin' to pull?"

But Cutteridge, smiling, gave him the eye and, when they got outside, declared in the nearest he could get to an apology, "We—myself and associates—don't know a thing about this place we are bound for. Some California horse doc sent me a skull and . . . well, I want you along as a kind of insurance."

"Skull," Jones said. "Chrissake, mister! You pullin' my leg?"

"According to Miles you're a good judge of whisky."

Jones, considering, rubbed a horny hand across the rasp of his chin. "There's a connection?"

"That'll depend on what we find when

we get there." Cutteridge leaned confidentially closer. "I know bones, but this head's got me puzzled. I want to see where it came from, talk to the fellow's neighbors—"

"You don't need me."

"Probably not," the man of science conceded, "but on the chance we're both wrong I'm prepared to pay two hundred a month —plus expenses, of course—for as long as you're willing to act in my behalf."

Jones distrustfully took hold of his head, stabbed a look both ways and peered again at Cutteridge as though fully expecting to find nobody there.

He swallowed, eyes sharpening. "Two hundred what?"

"United States dollars," Cutteridge smiled. "Coin of the realm."

Jones' glance jumped around again and Cutteridge laughed. "I've got all my marbles. You can check my credentials with the Bank of America or the Wells Fargo people. But," he said with one eye half closed, "when I employ a man, Jones, I expect to get my money's worth."

Jones should have given that statement a second look. He should have thought a while longer, but two hundred plus did not grow on any bushes he had passed to arrive at Redskin. And there was Big Ass Liz ready to pounce if he reneged. Still he couldn't quite convince himself there wasn't a joker in the woodpile someplace, having given up counting on Santa Claus before he'd got into his first long jeans. "What'd you say you did for a livin'?"

"Professor of vertebrate paleontology at one of the biggest schools in the East." Observing Yavapai's bemused expression, he said: "I guess you'd say I picked bones for a living."

Jones showed his surprise. It was dirty work, but every hide hunter he'd rubbed elbows with packed a roll big enough to choke a bull.

He stuck out a fist, then hastily retrieved it. "That manna from heaven falls rain or shine?"

"Regular as clockwork," Cutteridge assured him.

"I dunno," Jones said, turned suddenly cautious. "Sounds like fightin' wages to me."

"Do you get the impression I'm a man who'd plot murder?"

"Not murder, maybe, but . . ." Jones, eyes scrinched, put his head on one side. "You got a kind of deaconish look, but some of the deacons round these parts would skin a flea for its hide and tallow."

The professor looked pained. He declared with great patience, "It's a competitive world we live in today. Fellow in my position is bound to make enemies—and some pretty unscrupulous ones at that." He paused as though to gather his thoughts. "In the colorful jargon of this locality the kind of man I'm looking for, Jones, is someone who'll do to ride the river with. A man I can trust with my life, if need be."

Jones seemed impressed. He jerked his head in a solemn nod, though not so much to Cutteridge's clatter as to visions conjured of life with Liz should he fail to fall in with Cutteridge's plans. "Look no further," he said. "I'm your man," and grabbed the dude's paw in a bone-crushing grip. "When do we start?"

The scientist said, "You start right now. We're off to the railroad first thing in the morning," and let go of bruised knuckles to dig a fist in his pocket. He thrust some crumpled bills in Jones' hand. "Mr. Harragan goes with us. Lay in whatever we'll need for the trip and make sure I'm called no later than seven."

When the professor returned to the Knife & Arrow he was astonished to find the hotel's cramped lobby bulging at the seams with a miscellany of jaspers who all broke into voice the moment he was sighted. Mostly townsmen, they seemed, in workaday clothes with a belligerent sprinkling of red-shirted miners.

As the noise and confusion climbed toward bedlam Cutteridge, exasperated, raised both arms. "Just a minute! Hold your horses!" he cried through the hubbub. "Now then—*you*," he said, pointing his finger at a brawny Cousin Jack. "What is—"

"You ain't goin' t' git away with it! Nobody's takin' that coot outa camp without I'm paid ever' last cent he owes me!" Swearing, the big miner doubled huge fists amid a chorus of affirmative yells from the rest of them.

As the jostling throng packed closer around him, snarling and yapping like a pack of curs, Cutteridge's eye chanced to light on Pop Leddabrand, somewhat aloof at the foot of the stairs. The hash house proprietor, though obviously not in the best of spirits, did not—like the most of them —appear quite ready to tear him limb from limb.

"What's got into you people?" Cutteridge rasped, shaking an accusative finger at Pop. "I thought you were his friend, Mr. Leddabrand."

Hester's papa looked hard at him and spat. "When a woman grown sets her hat fer a man, you don't go round recitin' his shortcomin's or ferbid him the premises without you're honin' t' turn up a woods colt." The old man tucked a pinch of snuff behind his lip. "Now that he's run true t' form an' dropped her I aim t' git back a bit of my own."

"And what does that amount to?"

"Countin' meals, Bull Durham an' sundry etceteras I figger he's into me fer upwards of anyways one hundred dollars."

Cutteridge asked dryly, "Don't you want to tack on a buck or two for derailed dreams?"

"You may laff if you're a mind to but these folks he's taken advantage of has sent fer a rail an' all the fixin's. Without their claims is settled in full I expect things'll git a little rough around here."

Baldfaced blackmail—no doubt about it. But, staring into that sea of angry faces, Cutteridge reckoned this was one of those times when discretion might prove to be the

41

cheaper part of valor. It went sore against the grain to knuckle down to these rubes but he finally forced himself to ask, "How much will it take to get Jones off the hook?"

Leddabrand said with a wintry smile, "I would guess five hundred ought to turn him loose."

"I'll want pieces of paper marked 'paid in full' above the signatures of every man in this room," Cutteridge said. "You can be attending to that while I'm fetching my checkbook."

Christian's Camp, like companion diggings at Angel's and Altaville, was in those days considered an important community because of its location squarely in the center of California's expanding Mother Lode country. Upon arrival, shaken and racked by forty miles of staging after leaving the railroad, Cutteridge and Francie proceeded to sack out while Harragan and Jones— supposedly impervious to the rigors of the journey—were left with instructions to check out the facts concerning the skull and all persons known to have had any connection with it.

Forty-six hours later a conclave was held in Cutteridge's suite and the pooled information thoroughly sifted. Doctor Ralph Oglesbee, it appeared, was a popular physician, a firm believer in the Darwinian contentions and a part-time amateur paleontologist. He believed with others that man—when science had the rock-bottom facts—would be proved much older than was generally supposed. Another of his frequently voiced convictions held America to be the most probable cradle of prehistoric man. Proof of this conviction, according to general rumor, was the skull he had sent to Cutteridge's Boston office.

"It's old, all right," the professor admitted. "Opalized. Considerable specific gravity. Heavily encrusted. Gravel and shells both embedded. This camp is not unknown to archeologists. Paul Hubbs of Vallejo found part of a skull in dumped material from one of the mine shafts at Table Mountain—this was back before the war. Fool sawed it in half; part I didn't get went to those rattlebrains over at Philadelphia. They've found quite a bit of stuff under that mountain."

"That's not where this new skull come from," Jones tucked in, anxious to show that he had not been idle. "Some doc named Snell—he's over at Sonora—had a bunch of bones and other junk on display in his office he's supposed to have picked up round and about."

Cutteridge's stare advertised his disapproval. "You will have to learn, Jones, to be more precise. What exactly besides bones does he have?"

"Well, he don't exactly have nothin' no more—place burnt down," Yavapi told him. "One thing he had was a human jawbone, an' one of them hollered-out stones a lot of these Injuns used to grind corn in—"

"That's an artifact," the professor said sternly. "I'll thank you not to call artifacts 'junk.'"

It was probably the glasses gave him such a mean look; Jones hadn't seen him in specs before. He didn't much care for the tone of that, either. "I was only trying to help," he said, bristling.

"Of course he was, Daddy," Francie flew to his defense. "All this is new to him—after all, Rome wasn't built in a day. Yavapai will learn—"

"With that grandstander Mainson working night and day to discredit my findings," Cutteridge snapped, "we don't have all the time in the world. The science of fossils — you remember the Cardiff Giant, my dear, the hoax that cigar manufacturer carved out of gypsum, and the hundreds of thousands of credulous fools who rushed in with their dollars to see a prehistoric man before I branded it a fake? You just can't be too exact in this—"

"The skull Oglesbee sent you," Harragan declaimed, not minded to be left out when it came to kudos, "was dug from under Bald Mountain. Several miles away. At Altaville precisely."

Jones, regarding him testily, said: "It was discovered six months before the Doc got around to sendin' it to you. The mine it come out of has since been closed down. Shaft's filled with water."

Cutteridge considered this, intently thoughtful. "Well, well," he said, looking right through Jones, "so it's flooded now . . . no way to get into it."

"With the right kind of pumps," Harragan began, but Jones wasn't finished. "I've located the feller that dug it up; miner named Fletcher; well-known hereabouts."

Still with that speculative look in his eye Cutteridge, smiling as a sop to Jones' industry, said, getting up, "I believe we had better drop by and have a talk with him."

VI

FLETCHER DIDN'T mind discussing the matter. He appeared to have his facts firmly in mind. "When they was workin' this hole," he said, "we'd go down by a vertical shaft through black lava for about forty feet. And I don't think you'll git down there with pumps."

The workings, when they ran into borrasca, were 132 feet below the surface. "When we hit bedrock—looked like the bed of some old-timey river—we started a drift."

The river gravels, through the weight of centuries, appeared to have become more or less cemented from pressure and sunken bits of driftwood showed petrification. On this particular day Fletcher, noticing nothing different than usual, had gone to work at the end of the drift. "The gravel at this point was entirely cemented—nobody'd disturbed it. That skull, when I found it, was really embedded. I thought first off it was a chunk of petrified wood. I used my pick an' got it loose—grayish white it was. I knew it was a skull soon's I picked the thing up. It was all covered with this cementy stuff, see?"

He'd been shrewd enough not to chip any off. That night he'd taken it to the express office, turned it over to the agent, thinking some collector might be glad to get hold of it. Later that night someone had suggested Doc Oglesbee might want it. It had gone off in care of the stage driver, people from Alta and Angel's racing along to see what Doc would have to say about it.

Doc was plenty excited, being an ardent supporter of Darwin's thesis. "Boys," he cried, "this just knocks the hell out of old Moses!"

"There was even some newspaper stories about it," Fletcher remembered. "Oglesbee used to carry it around in his bag, showin' it even as far away as Amador—sure made food for a powerful lot of gassin'. He told everybody that would stand still to listen, it was nine hundred, ninety-four thousand, one hundred and thirty-four years older than Adam."

Cutteridge thanked Fletcher for his help. He seemed pretty well lit up himself and proposed a visit to Oglesbee straightaway, to find out, he said, precisely how Doc had arrived at that figure.

Jones demurred. "Some talk over at Angel's I think you oughta hear before you waste too much time with that hypothecator."

Cutteridge eyed him with an irascible scowl. "What kind of talk?"

"For Chrissake!" Harragan said, disgusted. But Cutteridge wasn't to be put aside. "What kind of talk?"

"Well, they're claimin' over there," Jones declared with a sour grin, "that skull come off a prospector fetched in from the hills, that they had it on display in one of their deadfalls and that somebody filched it off the back bar."

It stopped Cutteridge short with one foot off the ground. He had a look on his face like someone had stabbed him.

You could tell he was doing some furious thinking. "Don't you reckon," Jones slyly put it to Harragan, "it's time the Perfessor was brought up to date?"

Cutteridge may not have caught the words but something in the sound of them jerked his head up. "What's that?" he said, and Jones spread his hands. "As the boss of this clambake it don't seem quite right he should be keepin' things away from

48

you. Particular a thing like this Calaveras Man—"

The look Cutteridge wheeled on the *Transcript*'s correspondent was the kind no real man could stomach, Jones thought, without it came from his wife. Harragan, catching the full force of this glare, went from fish-belly white through the throes of his confusion into the deepest kind of purple before he got out, half strangled with fright and rage, "I—God damn it, she wouldn't *let* me! Said it would only up—"

"Who said?"

"Francie—"

"Show him the paper," Jones prompted, grinning.

Harragan reluctantly dragged it from his pocket. "Front page," Jones said as Cutteridge shook it open.

CALAVERAS MAN IDENTIFIED the headlines screamed, and in war scare type the subhead stated: ERNEST HENRY MAINSON CLAIMS BALD MOUNTAIN SKULL OF TERTIARY ORIGIN.

With livid cheeks and trembling hands Cutteridge read how the eminent paleontologist, Ernest Henry Mainson, from the City of the Bell, after carefully disembalming Fletcher's skull from its coating of an-

49

cient gravel and shells, had compared it under laboratory conditions with neanderthal and Gibraltar skulls, concluding from evidence examined that the find at Bald Mountain was infinitely older.

Its metamorphic state was then compared with petrification of wood fragments brought up from the Bald Mountain gravels, unquestionably contemporary. These gravels, the story went on, had already been dated by world famous geologist as belonging to the Tertiary Age. Said Mainson, *"They were sealed more unequivocably than the tombs of the Pharaohs under forty feet of solid lava."* Obviously then, Calaveras Man, as Fletcher's find was being called, could not be other than of similar antiquity. Also, Mainson pointed out, the mortar, jawbone and skull discovered several years earlier under nearby Table Mountain surely proved Man had not only existed in such remote times but had evolved a tool-shaping culture.

Cutteridge flung down the paper in a rage. "That son of a bitch!" he snarled through white lips, and Harragan quailed from the blaze of his stare. "What I want to know," Jones broke in, grimacing, "is how he got hold of that head in the first place." He said to Cutteridge, "I thought you claimed it was sent to your office."

"It was! The bastard bribed somebody—and it wouldn't be the first time he's stooped to skulduggery! The feller ought to be drummed out of—he's got no more scruples than . . . Not for nothing has that slippery conniver been called 'Foxy' Ernie!"

Jones, still with that suggestion of tantalizing merriment, said: "You don't have to take this layin' down."

Cutteridge, breaking off his tracking of Mainson's ancestry, came winging around like a bat out of Carlsbad. "I don't?"

"I'm just a poor country rube," Jones drawled, "that never got hardly past three times four. I dunno how much fact he's got back of him or how far you'd want to go with business, but if you'd like to pile him up in a heap . . ."

"Yes? Yes?" Cutteridge was all of a twitch to hear more. "If you can—"

"Couldn't you," Harragan asked, breaking in, "show that he took that skull from—"

The professor slammed him a look laced with lightning. "Are you out of your mind? He probably *hopes* I'll try that. You can be

51

sure if I did everybody concerned would swear they never heard of me!"

"It would cost him something," Jones said, interested. "How much would he pay to—?"

"Whatever he had to," Cutteridge muttered. "He's only got five or six million behind him! Don't you know that his father's Hugo Mainson, the Coal King, that tore up half of West Virginia. . . ." He considered Jones hopefully. "If you can dig up something that will make him look sick. . . ."

"We can try," Jones said, winking, and picked up his reins. "Harragan, let's go have a talk with a couple of fellers."

VII

ABOUT THE middle of the morning of the following day a boy came up from the railroad depot to Cutteridge's suite with a telegram. He had just finished reading it, was standing there thinking, when Francie—answering a knock at the door—let Harragan in.

"Well?" Cutteridge said, and Harragan, nodding, passed him three sheets of paper.

"Up half the night working on it," he growled.

The professor went over to better light by the window. He looked up, having read it, passed the sheets to Francie. "You think," he asked Harragan, "your paper will print it?"

"Will they ever! A thing like this—every wire service will carry it! They'll have Mainson hunting for a hole to crawl into!"

"It doesn't seem very dignified," Francie put in, and her father stood frowning.

"It's no skin off your nose," Harragan told him. "Only thing you've done is call it a fake. The press will love you—they'll have a field day with it!"

Cutteridge, passing him some currency, said: "Get Jones up here. Then go to the depot and book reservations through to Salt Lake—earliest possible."

Shortly after the correspondent left Jones walked in with a moonstruck smile in the direction of Francie who, touching up her hair, returned it brightly, much to her father's confused astonishment. "Jones," gruffed the great man, "take a look at this," and passed him the result of Harragan's labors.

Datelined "Christian's Camp," the story

suggested Mainson had been made the victim of a vicious bit of mining camp horseplay. The famous skull, according to Harragan, had never come out of a riverbed at all, but had been tongue-in-cheek lifted from a Indian burial off the side of a nearby mountain. Authority cited for this was a member of the clergy, Reverend Brier of Alvarado. According to Brier, his brother, a prospecting hardrock miner, had been on hand in the cave when the skull had begun its remarkable journey. Someone, apparently, had come up with the notion of giving it a coating of lime, shells and pebbles, whereupon it had been placed in the oven of a stove and baked for several days, after which it had been wedged in a prospecting drift under Bald Mountain awaiting Fletcher's "discovery." From thence, as related, it had gone to Doc Oglesbee, a self-confessed atheist, for presentation to Ernest Henry Mainson who had been conned into thinking it a genuine missing link. "Professor C. Culpepper Cutteridge, noted paleontologist and celebrated discoverer of the three-toed horse, when reached by this reporter—while extending warmest sympathy to his misled colleague—declared Calaveras Man 'as big a hoax as the Cardiff

Giant and the much-touted English Pilt-down Dawn Man."

"Well," Yavapai said, handing it back with a proprietory grin, "I reckon that ought to get him out of your hair. What's next on the docket? If you got nothin' on tap for the next couple days—"

"We're going to Salt Lake if we can get reservations; Harragan's over at the depot now. I've just had a telegram," Cutteridge informed him. "Brigham Young has asked me to call on him in connection with my discovery of *Equus parvulus*—the Three-Toed Horse," somewhat testily, noting Jones' expression.

"As a matter of fact," he went on, grimly frowning, "I'm not entirely sure but what I'd be wiser to ignore it. Back East I've been attacked by a lot of the clergy for teaching what these men of the cloth call 'godless evolution.'"

Jones, having nothing to say to that, unloaded a notion that was closer to his heart. "If we can't get tickets straightaway," he said, "how about givin' me a couple days off? I'd like to do some poking around over at—"

He was interrupted by a knock on the door. Harragan came in to say with a grimace, "No connections to be had before the fourteenth—"

"Why, that's two weeks away, pretty near!" exclaimed Cutteridge, sounding vexed. "Why can't—"

"I'm only repeating what I was told. I even went to the trouble of explaining who you were," Harragan said with some indignation. "We could book through to Wyoming straight off, it appears—"

"Then that's what we'll do," the scientist decided. "We'll go to Green River. Jones, see what you can pick up in the way of wagons and camp gear. That Green River plateau, I've been told, has some interesting fosils—"

"It's got a heap of hostile Injuns," Jones, cutting in, remarked sardonically. "You been told about them?"

Cutteridge waved that aside. "Get us tickets for as near to Green River as you can," he briskly told Harragan, "and accommodations for three wagons—wait, better make it five. . . . What do you think, Jones? Will we need the whole of one wagon for supplies?"

"I think," Jones said, looking down his nose, "we'd do better to pack in—mules," he explained for Francie's benefit. "Them hostiles is more partial to mule meat than—"

"Tell them six wagons," Cutteridge said to Harragan, and then, "Jones, you better start rounding them up."

"If we git jumped," Jones muttered, "you'll wish you had mules."

"You're bad as an old woman," Cutteridge declared, sounding put out. "Half the Indian troubles we read about are jumped-up affairs concocted by reporters out of no better reason than to sell a swath of papers. We're going to Green River. Now both of you get busy!"

They unloaded several days later in the desert country of the Green River plateau and, the following morning, headed south. Cutteridge found it pretty slow progress and put several "bugs" into Yavapai's ear. Jones, whose boiling point was at best rather low, finally hauled off, exasperated, to declare with some heat, "We'd of made better time if you'd taken my advice. Since you didn't an' we're stuck with these goddam wagons—"

"I'll thank you to watch your language, Jones. My daughter has had the benefit of—"

"Don't be stuffy," Miss Francie admonished, coming up in her Boston riding clothes and bowler. "Mr. Jones isn't interested in my education," she remarked in her dulcet templebells tinkle, brightly eying the recipient of her largess. "What Daddy means," she interpreted for him, "is how could he have brought his bones back on mules? Without the wagons we might as well not have come." And she smiled to take the sting from her words.

"But this ain't buffalo country, Miss Francie."

Her face puckered prettily. The pansy eyes opened wide in astonishment. "Buffalo? But Daddy isn't after buffalo, Yavapai."

Jones, peering suspiciously, yanked off his rattlesnake-banded disreputable hat to sleeve off the drip coming out of his hair. "He ain't?"

"Of course not. It's fossils he's hunting —didn't you know?"

Jones scratched his head. "Fossils, ma'am?" He couldn't have looked more confused if she'd stood on her head and waggled her toes.

"Things you dig out of the ground," she explained, and rolled up the black velvet of two pansy eyes as though casting about for some way of putting it that even a moron might recognize. "Relics of animals, people or plants from past geological ages, you know . . . like footprints or ferns . . . things that have been a long time dead. Like that skull of Fletcher's."

"Oh!" Jones stared distrustfully from one to the other. *"Them* kinda bones! Why didn't he say so?"

Unable to find a tactful rejoinder, Francie, in the tone of a wistful supplicant, put the problem squarely between them. "From what General Miles was telling us, Yavapai, we thought you would know where Daddy could find some."

"Well . . ."

"It's terribly important," she urged, reaching out to rest a hand on his arm. "You see, Daddy's job at the university depends more than you would imagine on what he is able to turn up in the field. He made a truly great find in the three-toed horse, but with all this uproar over Darwin's—"

"He wouldn't understand Darwin," he father cut in. "Good lord, girl, the fellow's—"

"There is a place north of here," Jones remembered, flushed by the feel of that hand upon his arm. "The Judith Basin, and a heap better place to be right now with all these redskins diggin' up the hatchet. There's acres of bones up there; all kinda bones. Injuns call 'em thunder horses."

Cutteridge pricked up his ears at that. "Where is this place?" he demanded brusquely.

Jones dragged his stare off the girl with reluctance. "Montana," he said, "but to get there from here would take five-six weeks messin' round with these wagons. There's places we'd have to take 'em plumb apart, mebbe hoist 'em up three hundred foot cliffs an'—"

"There's nothing around here? I thought this Jim Bridger country—"

"Sure there's bones here," Jones said with a snort, "but there's a sight more Injuns an' they're fed up with whites. These bones more important to you than your hair?"

The professor shot an irritated look toward his daughter. "I am sure the danger is considerably exaggerated. I came out here for fossils and I intend to go back with some. Of course, if you're afraid . . . ?"

Jones seemed a bit irritated himself. He chewed on his cheek for a while, shrugged his shoulders. "I guess I can stand it if you can," he growled. "We'll have to go back to Green River an' start over. We haven't got a quarter of the gear we'll need. An' we better have some help if what you're figurin' is to fill these wagons."

VIII

THE TOWN of Green River in those halcyon days of the early '70s was the outfitting center for a considerable territory, supplying among others the mines and prospects of the Sweetwater region some eighty miles north. During the past several years some ten thousand persons had come stampeding into Wyoming, tearing up God's handiwork, gouging and carousing, establishing such mushrooming communities as South Pass City, Atlantic City and Miner's Delight. Now these camps were playing out and dispirited hardrock men were tramping the streets of Green River trying to find ways of filling their bellies.

In a town crammed with masterless men Jones had no trouble securing a crew for the manual labor of Cutteridge's enterprise. He bought more wagons, teams and tools and, inside of a fortnight, the Cutteridge bone haulers moved from the status of something to goggle at to a sight more commonplace than drunken Indians. The gigantic skulls, some with horned protuberances of astonishing ferocity, which Jones' teamsters fetched into town to be packed into boxcars for shipment to Boston, appeared to groan through Green River in a never-ending stream.

Jones had other chores which had not been enumerated as being among his duties when the great man had taken him under his wing. He had become quite proficient as a boss excavator and all-around factotum. He still couldn't define the finer shades of relationship among the Mosassuria and other dragons the professor's army of hard-rock rehabilitates were busily unearthing in bewildering profusion, but he had a sharp eye for the things that counted and his general appearance—like the bonehandled pistol that flopped at his groin—stood Cutteridge in good stead on more than one historic occasion. Jones was the professor's ambassador to the Philistines, a first class persuader. One look at the cold wintry glimmer of an unwinking stare above outthrust jaw and belt braced hands generally substantiated the rightness of whatever notion Cutteridge came up with. It softened opposition not unlike the way a hot knife slides through butter.

Nor was Harragan afforded any greater degree of leisure. An avalanche of communiques was expected daily of his industrious pen. The world was kept in constant touch with the multiple marvels of the Cutteridge discoveries, and whenever the news appeared in temporary danger of tapering off Jones' inventiveness would fill the gap. The professor might not shine on missing links when it came to man's own personal evolution, but with beasts of the field and reptiles any child would know after reading the *Transcript's* on-the-spot coverage there was no greater digger at work in the universe than Yr humble servant, C. Culpepper Cutteridge.

Perhaps in the dim lonely watches of some star-filled night with the coyotes' yammer drifting through the brush Jones may briefly have been reminded of the girl he'd left behind, but his days were filled with bones and Francie. That he had few chances to work up any passes could not be charged to lack of inclination, though he did rather tend to suffer apprehensions which had not interfered with his prowess as of yore. She *was* a bit different, no getting around that, and uncommon adroit at avoiding situations where the sap in a man might be at all encouraged to get out of hand.

And then one day, from endeavors elsewhere, Ernest Henry Mainson apeared at Green River with a hungry eye, a crew of diggers and his own private staff of press correspondents.

Cutteridge, not unnaturally, was considerably shook up to find his most pertinacious rival camped—as Jones put it "right on his shirttail" and breathing down his neck. To describe him as outraged would be the mildest of understatements. He was furious, bellicose, and discernibly apprehensive.

"We've got to get rid of this fellow at all costs. He's the most unscrupuous claim jumper in Wyoming! Give him an inch and he'll do me straight out of—Harragan! Get off a dispatch to that rag of yours at once —see if you can't get it on the wire services. But be careful how you word it. He'll sue if you give him the ghost of a chance, but I want him shown up for the conniving poacher we know him to be! The fellow's worse than a plague of cicadas," he told

Jones as Harragan dashed off to spread a true picture. "Nothing's sacred to that vulture—nothing! He's come out here to do me a meanness. You'll see!"

Jones thought a while. "Has he got a strong gut?"

"He's got more gall than a horde of brass monkeys!"

According to scientific practice, it appeared, to receive credit as discoverer of any new species one had first to publish its description through channels or deliver a paper before one of the more acceptable learned societies. Mainson didn't boggle to take his claims directly to the press. To him discovery was all and on more than just a handful of occasions—according to Cutteridge—this unspeakable fellow had received press recognition for other people's discoveries; and this was what the professor was afraid of.

Especially after that business of Fletcher.

"You know what he does?" the professor said righteously. "These private collectors seldom have either the opportunity or entrée to get their finds recognized. Mainson keeps an army of scouts busy round the clock locating these amateurs. Then he pays 'em a visit and in no time at all he's talked them round—he could talk a she-bear out of its cubs!"

"What do you mean, he talks them around?"

Cutteridge, gritting his teeth, grimaced bitterly. "Make the fools think he's doing them a favor! With the devil's own charm he identifies the species in their collections. If they've found anything new he fits these into some niche in biology, names them suitably, describes them in print and credits himself with their discovery. You'd think they'd learn to keep their treasures away from him, but no. These backwoods teachers and regions historians positively dote on that pirate! I mean it! They never seem to recognize how gullible they've been. Then even scout stuff out for him, ship him new finds, only to be defrauded of their kudos all over!"

Jones clucked in sympathy. "Too bad you can't happen onto a few of them."

Cutteridge peered sharply, but Jones' face was too bland to suggest censure or sarcasm. "I could never do that kind of thing," Francie's father declared primly. And Francie said, "If we could just tie his hands for another six weeks. . . ."

And Jones, looking fatuous, tugged at his

moustache. "I'll see what I can do," he sighed, getting up. "If you only *could*," Francie cried, dewy-eyed.

At the door Cutteridge said, voice thick with loathing, "It isn't so much for myself I'm alarmed—you have to understand what's back of this business. Turning up here—knowing his methods . . . Everything that fellow can get his hands on goes back to Philadelphia!"

He made it sound the worst crime imaginable.

With a kind of shudder, staring off into space, he said in tones that were damp with pity, "Several years ago my uncle, one of your real old-fashioned philanthropists, out of the kindness of his heart endowed the University with a splendidly modern and, regrettably, rather pretentious museum building which—if Mainson keeps on at the pace he's going—will leave my school with the best of facilities and nothing of relative value to put into it."

He seemed, Jones thought, pretty near beside himself. And Francie looked about to burst into tears.

"To truly appreciate," Cutteridge sighted, "the kind of frauds this fellow will instigate I'll give you an instance. Until just recently he and his field crew have been plundering Missouri, stripping it of fossils —helter-skelter as a bull in a china shop. On one occasion he had the gall to not only name but positively identify twenty-one different species of dinosaur by nothing more than a handful of teeth!

"Last year, near the Colorado border, he found projecting from a cutbank the weathered skull of a monstrous creature which he identified on the spot as a relative of the Mosassuria. Now this group of marine reptiles, you understand, had originally been found in rock beds adjacent to the Maas River in Holland. Mainson's Butte Creek discovery, because of size and other criteria, he decided to be not only a new species but a new genus as well. Uncovered, the vertebrae proved to extend fully seventy-five feet. Of course, this length by itself made the find remarkable. Its most notable feature, however, appeared to be a long snake-like neck—this was longer than the rest of its body, tail included. When he found these remains they were not, you understand, articulated. This gigantic skeleton had, through the years, somewhat fallen apart. It was all there, however, and the newspaper people made a great to-do over it. I was so impressed by the accounts I had read I went to Philadelphia to look at it myself."

The professor paused to catch breath and grimace. "Of course, the moment I saw it I burst into laughter. I simply could not restrain myself. Mainson had named it *Elasmosaurus platyurus*, but he'd put the head on the wrong end, you see."

Jones, whacking his thigh, let go of a belly laugh. But it struck the wrong note in the gloom of this conference called to find some way to stop Foxie Ernie.

Squaring his jaw he told Francie, sobering, "I'll scout around an' see what I can come up with."

IX

LOCATING MAINSO's headquarters, Jones— after loosening the gun in his holster—paid him a visit which, for brevity, transcended even Cutteridge's rush at time.

Expecting, from all he had heard about the man, to be sneeringly confronted with some slavering bully wreathed in fire and brimstone, Jones on being ushered into the presence stood flinty-eyed peering about him suspiciously. "It's Foxy Ernie I've come here to see," he told the immaculate gentleman who stood up, graciously smiling, to put out a hand.

"I expect that's me," this apparition laughed, using the ignored hand to indicate a chair. "Won't you sit down, Mr. Jones?"

He was younger than Cutteridge by at least seven years, polished, urbane and—though dressed in the sober garb of a Quaker—more resembling in face and gestures the sort of French count one finds in sophisticated comedies. His eyes twinkled amiably. "I see you've fetched along your gun to bear the lion in his den."

Jones, plainly out of countenance, growled, "*You're* Ernest Mainson?"

"It's the name I find on most of my mail. What's old Cutty got up his sleeve now? Don't be so stiff, man. Sit down and let's discuss this like something other than a pair of strange dogs."

Jones took a closer look at him. Beneath the fine manners and undeniable charm this feller had a lot more than hot air going for him. That whimsical stare didn't come from the eyes of any drawing room jumping jack. His kind of confidence wasn't going to dent easily.

Still ignoring the chair, Yavapai said

sparely, "I can git it said quicker if I stay on my feet. We may not have any patent on this basin but we've got possession an' by Gawd we're going' to keep it. With bullets if we have to!" And without another word he took his departure.

Mainson pulled out of Green River the next day.

The next word Harragan brought of his doings, he was camped at Haystack Butte in the Washakie Basin maintaining courier service with the telegraph line to speed his claims of new species to a waiting world. He carried, Harragan reported, a Greek lexicon around with him to better enable him to furnish on the spot names like *Dicornutus*, *Bifurcatus*, *Loxolophodon* and *Expressicornis* to the things he dug up and crated for shipment. A brass key pounder who had just sent off a dispatch from Cutteridge poured oil on the fires of their inveterate enmity by erroneously transmitting Mainson's Loxolophodon as a repeat of Cutteridge's Lefalophodon.

Cutteridge promptly accepted credit for both, declaring Mainson's fossil was his own *Tinoceras* discovered last year. Mainson, furious, came back with the charge Cutteridge was publishing the names of critters dredged from a feverish imagination, after-wards using them to claim priority when anything likely showed up in Mainson's camp. They hurled names at each other with alarming impunity and all this, of course, sold a raft of papers, printed and reprinted in thirteen different languages.

Cutteridge then heard again from Brigham Young. He brooded over this for a couple of days, at last summoning Jones and Harragan to conference. "We're about through here at Bridger anyway," he growled, striding energetically across the faded carpeting. "With all those clergymen back East hollering I'm a little reluctant to place myself in such a stronghold of cant as Salt Lake City.

"Unfortunately, however, with so many bible pounders already popping their buttons to crucify me I'm in very poor shape to antagonize with impunity a person as influential as the man who stands in the bell-tower of Mormonism." He peered first at his daughter, then at his disciple from the world of printer's ink. Finally he got around to looking at Jones. "I'm afraid we're going to have to go over there."

It was Francie who said, "I don't believe we can afford to ignore him, working this close to his own headquarters. What do you think, Yavapai?"

Jones, thus appealed to, put on his dying calf look and tossed his hat in the corner. "I ain't never known Mis Francie," he said, coloring, "to be anythin' but right."

"Harragan?"

"I'll go along with that."

"Very well, then. We'll pack up the rest of these fossils, run them into town and—"

"Hold on," Jones growled.

They all stared, puzzled.

"Old Brigham's a pretty big bug when it comes to that Utah patch of potatoes. You wanta traipse over there lookin' like something the cat dragged in? Mormons is people just like anyone else."

Cutteridge scowled. "What's that supposed to mean?"

"You don't know what he wants. But one thing you can bank on: he ain't over partial to Gentiles at best. I think you better make some noise about this."

The professor still didn't get it, but Harragan's eyes had begun to light up. "Sure —tell the world!"

"That's what I'd do," Jones nodded. "Send him a wire. Let the papers know you're on the way. Make a big splash.

'YOUNG SENDS FOR CUTTERIDGE. CUTTERIDGE TO VISIT SALT LAKE' —that kinda thing. Hell, you're a big potater, too, Perfesser. Play it up! Arrive with horns tootin''. Ever' wagon crammed with bones—put on a few extra. Give 'em a parade, somethin' to shout about."

Francie said, "Yes! You don't have to knuckle down to nobody, Daddy!"

One thing about Cutteridge. You didn't have to hammer him over the head to make him see reason when it accrued to his advantage.

They arrived in the Mormon stronghold like Marco Polo coming home from his travels, whips popping, outriders flanking the long string of wagons, Miss Francie up front on a white horse beside Daddy, their tame correspondent riding on his other side, derby hat, yellow shoes and all, this vanguard followed a couple of horse-lengths behind by Yavapai Jones in his broken-rimmed headgear flanked by two Indians in full paint and feathers.

Nor was Salt Lake laggard with its own demonstration. Gay bits of bunting decorated the storefronts; the walks were jammed with waving people, all of them

74

shouting, not a few of them grinning from ear to ear. Kids ran along the sides of the procession and Brigham Young himself with a bevy of bishops came out of the Temple to welcome the bone hunters and publicly extend them the seal of approval and show the whole world all the clergy weren't bigots, that the Latter Day Saints of Jesus Christ weren't asleep at the switch when it came to hard facts.

If Cutteridge still entertained a few doubts he hid them well. His smile was benevolent—he even waved to the kiddies, took one of them up on the neck of his pony. He was all dressed up for this special occasion in an outfit Buffalo Bill would have envied—even a pair of fringed gauntlets and a cream colored Stetson that set him back sixty dollars. He wasn't a showman, but Francie made up for whatever he lacked, looking smart as a queen in her Boston riding garb, radiant, Jones thought, as a ten dollar diamond.

"Welcome to Salt Lake," Brigham Young said in greeting. "It isn't every day we can shake a hand that has so eloquently defended the Faith."

Cutteridge's party, of course, didn't know what he was talking about; for that matter neither did Cutteridge who was not the greatest worker in any religious vineyard. But—if, like Jones, he secretly wondered—he took it in stride, grimacing dutifully, putting the best face he could on the matter.

There was a deal of fidgeting, some restless milling, as hot air continued to be pumped by both sides without any evidence of a looked-for letup. Mopping the sweat off his neck and chin, Jones, sotto voce, growled at Harragan, "See you later."

"Here—where you going?"

"Hi gollies, I'm goin' to git me a drink!"

"Salt water?"

"Salt hell!"

The reporter said, wistful, "These people don't hold with nothing stronger'n birch beer."

"You don't know the right people," Yavapai grinned and standing not upon the order of his going, took off.

Harragan, swearing, peered after him enviously. He'd have given a pretty to be as heedless as Jones. But he had a soft job with pay from two sources and long months of catering to it held him resentfully in his tracks.

The horses, glad of the rest as the ox

teams, stood hipshot, lethargically switching flies off their hides. A salty breeze came up off the lake. A brass band played a few rousing hymns and the official ceremonies came to an end. Their business, the cleric said, would be discussed, God willing, on the morrow; meanwhile one of the bishops would show them where to camp.

The bishop assigned had a stern Spartan's face, and more the brisk manner of a centurion, Harragan thought, than seemed normal in a man of the cloth.

Cutteridge looked around for Jones, asked Francie if she had seen him. She looked around, too. Harragan could have told them, if not where the scout was, at least what he'd gone after, but—though considerably tempted—prudently refrained, not for the sake of Jones or the bishop but out of deference to Cutteridge's local standing.

He did, however, tell Cutteridge later.

The professor said, "Well, it's a common enough failing. We can't all be saints. Long as it doesn't interfere with his work—"

"That's just the point," the reporter growled, scowling. "Who is to say? If he goes on one of these toots when we're out in the field . . ."

"We'll cross the bridge when we come to it."

"But these Indians, sir—he could get us all massacred!"

Cutteridge chopped that off with finality. "Our red brothers, Harragan, are doing their level best to get along. I am sick of this newspaper Indian scare talk. Treat them right, they'll treat you the same way —that's all you have to remember about Indians. I recommend for you study the Golden Rule. There's a lot of sound sense in the Bible, Harragan."

X

THE BIG audience with Brigham came off behind closed doors the next day. Harragan, as a working member of the press, was not invited.

The professor, distinctly uneasy now that he had gotten right down to it, attended with some trepidation, understandably nervous as to what had inspired a man of Young's caliber to summon into this stronghold of religion any part of an expedition bent on proving the Darwinian theory. Since Francie's presence had not been solicited he arrived like a prodded tiger with none to fall back on but reticent Jones.

Ringer by his council of sober church dignitaries the top man in Utah wasted no time beating around through the tules but came at once, cool and bluntly, to the point.

The *Book of Mormon,* it turned out, was under fire in certain quarters because it placed horses in early America while accepted data in the guise of facts held Spanish colonizers and explorers responsible for bringing horses to these shores, and no longer ago than the 16th century.

"But," said Brigham, "if—as reported— you have found bones of horses antedating the arrival of these Spanish adventurers obviously the *Book* is proved to be correct."

It was at this point in the proceedings, while the pause built up with significance and pressure, that Cutteridge got that white look about the gills and commenced sweatily to look for some hole he might crawl into.

One of the elders cleared his throat. "And have you, in fact," he demanded impatiently, "found such bones or has the report, like most of the things one reads in the papers, been grossly exaggerated?"

The professor, still palpably uneasy, said

with noticeable care: "I've found a considerably quantity of horse bones which go back many years beyond the advent of Spaniards."

No doubt about this being what they wanted to hear. The whole room seemed to brighten. A few smiles, even, appeared about to blossom, but Cutteridge was not through. Holding up his hands to still the starting clamor, "I think," he said, "it should be pointed out the fossils I've unearthed are of *Equus parvulus*, a three-toed horse, not precisely the kind envisioned today as being hitched to a plow or wagon."

The insipient smiles disappeared. Though Brigham appeared inclined to brush aside this addenda, four or five of the dignitaries, one couldn't help noticing, were beginning to exchange rather sober glances. Thinking to be helpful, Jones, speaking into the vacuum, said, "We've got several crates of them bones in the wagons."

Some of the sterner looks thawed a little, though Cutteridge himself provided little evidence of sharing this comfort. When one of the elders inquired, "May we see them?" he reluctantly nodded. "I'd better tell you right now they don't look much like horses—I mean the horses you're accustomed . . . They're not much larger than jackrabbits, gentlemen."

Quite a hubbub broke out among the shocked faces, but the bishops backed Brigham who, drawing a hand down the length of his beard, said to Cutteridge: "Just answer this with a plain yes or no. Did horses exist in North America prior to the advent of Spaniards?"

The professor said, "Yes," and everyone drew a satisfied breath.

Then Brigham wanted to know if Cutteridge would publicly proclaim this fact, in effect if he would endorse it?

The professor said, "Certainly," and the meeting broke up with the bone hunters being given the keys to the city. As Cutteridge told Harragan later, "I was not prone to look a gift hippus in the mouth."

It was decided to accept the Mormon hospitality and take a week off to give the expedition's workers a chance to rest up, get their dirty clothes laundered and afford all hands a bit of recreation. This news was received by the crew with some grumbling for, as one of them told Jones, "You can't even spit in this golrammed town without

layin' yourself open to fines an' imprison-
ment!'' But Jones had been to Salt Lake
before. He understood what really was
bothering these fellers and gave them the
benfit of past experience. Thereafter they
weren't too often underfoot.

It wasn't so easy for him to unwind. Harragan was kept busy filing dispatches. Jones
found himself with too much time on his
hands. The professor made it plain that, as
part of management, he was not to attempt
any of the pastimes which, indulged in by
the expedition's flunkies, might be reluctantly overlooked.

The most excitement he got out of the
visit came unheralded and unwanted the
night he took Francie to a music hall performance, and it wasn't a kind of excitement
a man would hope to sample again.

The bill featured jugglers and high-wire
artists, a barbershop quartet, a third rate
magician and a female contralto that turned
out to be the highlight of the performance.
She was a splendid looking creature in a
black lace gown with hair like a golden halo
coiffured in an upsweet mop that looked in
constant danger of tumbling apart but
somehow never did. She sang several songs
that were currently popular and then, for a

encore, *The Harp That Once Through Tara's Hall*, *The Little Box of Pine* and *Just Before the Battle, Mother*. Even Francie conceded she was "pretty good for a half-trained voice."

"You know," Jones said as they made their way back to the wagon encampment. "That girl sure reminds me of somebody," and he looked just as puzzled as he sounded.

"What girl?"

"That song singer—"

"Are you still thinking about *her?*" Francie sounded rather considerably put out and reckoned she had some right to be seeing how little attention he'd paid since catching his first startled look at that taffytop. It was the first time in a rather extensive experience that her arsenal of weapons had proved insufficient to hold a man's attention. "Really, Jones, sometimes . . . *You aren't hearing a word I say!*"

It was nearer the truth than any squire of dames should ever let a girl get without he was honing for a whole heap of trouble. Yavapai, starting guiltily, jerked up his head. "Lord, Miz Francie, that just ain't so," he gulped, copiously striving to pick up the thread of that abandoned conversation. "It—it—" He pretty near had to run to keep up with her.

Chin in the air, eyes straight ahead, she said in the choked-up tones of trust betrayed, "I don't care to hear any more about it."

They went the rest of the way in a stomping silence that would have made his ears ache if he hadn't been so taken up with the inexplicable puzzle of that music hall nightingale. The lights had been too poor from where they had sat to disentangle her features, but certain gestures, a certain something in the lines of that black sheathed body when taken in conjunction with her canary-yellow hair had struck mighty hard at some chord of memory, and the vibrations therefrom wouldn't let him alone.

He spent a bad night and first thing the next morning before Francie and Daddy had even thought of getting up he saddled a horse and set out for downtown.

The music hall when he got there was locked up and deserted. But the cook at the all-night diner to which his missed camp breakfast eventually took him allowed there'd be someone around about ten. So he dawdled a while over a second cup of java and, when he could stand the suspense no longer, got back on his horse and went round there again.

The place was still closed.

He got off his horse and squatted down to build a smoke. His thoughts were too preposterous, too disturbing for any lengthy contemplation. Tossing away his half smoked Durham he went over to stare at the bill of last night's performance still pasted to a board beside the ticket window. And there it was, plain as paint: MISS MAISEE DEVEREAUX, THE COLORADO SONGBIRD.

While he was staring a sharply dressed gent drove up in a hack, paid off the driver and, getting out a ring of keys, approached the door. Jones watched him unlock it.

Scowling, he said, "Don't suppose you'd know where I could find that girl singer you had here last night?"

The man with the keys, without even so much as throwing a look at him, declared, "That's right," and pulled open the door.

"Look, Mac," Jones said, catching hold of his arm, "this is powerful important. To me, anyway."

"The whole company left last night on the train." He shook off Jones' hand. Then, relenting, said "You an uncle or something?"

"Yeah," Jones grunted. "You wouldn't know where they've gone?'

The man considered him again. "Ain't gone nowhere. Track washed out ten miles down the line. They're going to have to stay over. . . . No, I can't say where she's put up. Wasn't staying with the rest of that bunch; but we're holding them over. If it's that important to you, come back tonight. Maybe you can pick her up after the show."

Jones chewed his lip. "Can I buy a ticket now, some-place well up toward the front?"

"We don't sell reserved seats. Your best chance, Jack, is to be here early and get early through the door."

Yavapai, thanking him, rode back to camp. But he was far too disquieted to hang around long. While the sun was still a good four hours above the lake he went back to town to take up a stand before the deserted ticket booth.

After a time he began to feel hungry but chewed on a frazzled end of his moustache rather than chance losing his place at the window.

Time sure crawled.

He was batting away at a persistent horse fly when the first arrivals from the performing company went on around to the rear of the theater. A man came with a girl and unlocked the front door but closed it behind them.

Another twenty minutes dragged itself down the drain toward oblivion. Jones killed the fly with a lucky swipe and, hearing a hack, looked up in time to see a man help a yellow haired girl from the vehicle and, with her, set out for the hall's back door.

Jones stared with dropped jaw, his apprehensions confirmed. It just didn't seem possible, but if that wasn't Hester Leddabrand from Redskin traipsing off with that dandy he sure didn't know up from down anymore!

XI

HE WATCHED them through a kind of red haze while the gorge of outrage rose in his throat at this evidence of perfidy. How fickle, he wondered, could a frail get to be in eleven short months! And her a small-town girl besides, daughter of a backwoods hash house keeper!

It sure brought the old Adam up in Jones. As they disappeared, laughing, heads close together and hand in hand around a corner of the building, seething, furious, he took out after them in jackrabbit jumps.

He got to the stage entrance just in time to hear the back door click shut. Coming up, panting, he gave it a yank that nearly tore his arm off. When it finally got through to him the thing was locked he commenced banging on it with the butt of his six-shooter, making enough noise to raise the dead.

A beefy broken-nosed character with cauliflower ears threw it open with a scowl. "What's all the racket, Jack?"

"That dame! Hester Ledda—"

"Ain't no Hesters in this place, buddy. Now clear out—scat! Before I wrop that gun round yer teeth an' lower them ears t' where they'll do you fer wings."

Jones, seeing the bulk of him, put away his hogleg. "Maisee!" he cried, digging the name from the whirl of his thoughts. "That's it! Maisee—that singer!"

"Wot abaht 'er?"

"I've got to see—"

"She yer wife?'

"Well . . . no. But—"

"Then you can come round with the rest

of these Johnnies. After the show," Bat Ears sneered, and shut the door.

Jones heard the lock and used some pretty foul language until he ran out of breath. But the door stayed shut and, gnashing his teeth, he tramped around to the front to find a long line of patrons queued up before the window.

In his indignation he was minded to go back to camp and find a dog to kick. He even turned clear around to go hunt up his horse but somehow, instead, presently found himself shuffling along in the line that was inching its way toward admission.

He thought, by grab, the show would never be over, but in the fullness of time it finally was. He was out of his seat before the last curtain, hurrying around to the door she'd gone in through, but others, apparently, had had the same notion. He was fifth to parade his scowls and bristling, poorest dressed of the lot in his broken-rimmed Stet hat and dusty range clothes.

Two of the others had their arms full of flowers and one had a big candybox under his arm. The fourth, like Jones, had just fetched himself but was dressed to the nines in his best bib and tucker. You had just so much choice in a getup like that; the guy had to be either a undertaker, gambler or a goddam dude.

Jones gave this feller the bulk of his attention. Them Greeks bearing gifts didn't rate a second glance but the self-assured sneers of that long drink of water got under his skin like a hideful of peach fuzz. "Are you waiting for someone?" this Lochinvar asked behind the façade of a withering arrogance.

"No," Jones said, putting on a sour grin, "I just come round to tell you bo-peeps the lamb you're huntin' just left by the front."

With looks of consternation bordering on betrayal the three luggage toters took off at a run, but the silk hatted dandy with a thin snort of laughter shot his cuffs and stayed put.

Yavapai glowered. He made a fist and held it up where in the light from the door lamp the black garbed dude could see it.

All it got him was a sneer.

"I've a good mind," Jones said, advancing belligerently, "to give you somethin' to remember me by."

With no hint of perturbation the supercilious dude stood fast in his tracks, not even bothering to put up his dukes. He looked —if anything—to be rather enjoying this.

Jones, disconcerted, floundered to a stop.

As though on cue the door was flung open. The broken nosed ex-pug, coming out to hook it back, ignoring Jones completely, touched his cap to the dude and grunted, "Said to tell yer she'll be along in a jiffy."

Yavapai, scowling, settled into his tracks.

Bat Ears returned to his stool inside. The dude, paying no attention to Jones now, brushed some non-showing lint from a sleeve of his tailed coat, straightened a tie that was impeccable and, whistling a few off-key bars from *Rustle of Spring,* looked indescribably bored.

Jones tried again to think how he might get rid of him but Hester appeared before he'd caught up with any solution.

In the light from the lamp above the door she looked regal as any pictured queen. Brushing past Jones as though he were some loathsome beggar she said, "Hugo! How nice of you," and reached to take his proffered arm.

"Just a minute there, missy!" Jones thrust out a hand that grasped nothing but air. Hugo, moving up expectantly, said, "Is this fellow bothering you?" And Hester, cool as a well chain, asked, "Was he speaking to me?"

The door man stuck his head out to watch.

Yavapai's face was something to see. No pulque-drunk squaw could have looked more furious or more mixed-up. Shutting his mouth with a slap of teeth he bowed his back to say with a beller: "Don't give me that hoity-toity talk! You knew me good enough back at Redskin when—"

Though a trifle flushed she said "Oh!" cool enough. "I remember you now . . . the fellow they were going to ride out on a rail. The one who left in such a hurry after some-one paid his debts he didn't even stop to tell his girl goodbye."

XII

WITH EVERY report brought in by Harragan to the Cutteridge wagon camp Mainson was ranging farther afield, buying up private collections, putting out new crews of diggers and turning up fresh discoveries. Cutteridge, like most of those persons truly interested, was a collector—he wanted the whole thing, every bone complete. Mainson's great drive was concerned with discovery, something new and different. Time and again he would stake his reputation on some fabulous monster which promptly clothed with gargantuan flesh on what Cutteridge and the academicians considered mighty trifling evidence. A gambler at heart he had the luck of the devil.

Cutteridge, in considerable alarm lest the indefatigable Ernest Henry should succeed in gobbling every publicity worthy fossil still moldering underground, called Yavapai on the carpet in no uncertain fashion. With Francie hovering over his shoulder to translate any obscure phases of Daddy's apprehension, the professor told him straight from the shoulder: "We've got to get moving!"

Jones, neck deep in the wounds inflicted by his recent run-in with old Pop Leddabrand's burgeoning daughter, appeared too wrapped in the tatters of self-pity to have much concern for the imminent catastrophe threatening his employer. But Cutteridge woke him up in short order.

"You've learned enough about the way the world spins to understand how precarious are the seats of the mighty. To stay in the limelight of public acclaim one needs a bit more to rest upon these days than the things he was able to accomplish yesterday. Universities, Jones, are no less fickle than the smiles of the multitude. Sensation seekers, voracious for kudos!"

He paused to glare. "I suggest you pay a reasonable attention or, before you know it, you are likely to find yourself back in Redskin cleaning out spittoons for that pistol-packing harridan! Do I make myself clear?"

"What do you want from me?" Jones growled, grimacing.

"A new location! Some place unscratched by that upstart's myrmidons where we've some chance to outshine the frantic hoorah stirred up by this Quaker charlatan!"

"Daddy," Francie told Jones earnestly, "needs to get his name back onto the front pages. Harragan's a genius"—she tossed the *Transcript's* man a flurried flash of teeth—"but even the wildest inventiveness these days just can't keep up with concrete facts. What we honestly need is a miracle, but I imagine Daddy will settle for a reasonable facsimile. Ferocious colossals are Mainson's stock in trade. What we've got to have is something more ferocious, or—"

"What about the Judith Basin?"

Cutteridge peered down his nose. "What about it?"

"I guess," Jones said, "I shouldn't of mentioned it."

"Why not?" Cutteridge pounced.

"Expect you'd find it a little *too* wild, all these Injuns wavin' their hatchets . . ."

"Yes?" Francie said. Even Harragan appeared to prick up his ears.

Yavapai frowned as the professor gave over his tour of the room to stand squinting up at him, opening and shutting his pudgy fists like the gills of a fish too long out of water. "Be no place," Jones said, squinting back, "for people that's been raised up in a city."

"But there's bones?" Francie prodded.

"Oh, there's bones enough to furnish a slaughter pen. Acres an'—"

Cutteridge's nose began to twitch like a rabbit's. "Where is this place? How soon can we get there?"

Mainson, last heard from, had been over in New Mexico scratching at the Puerco and Torrejon formations, ultimately to prove of very real scientific importance, overlaying as they did the dinosaur beds of Cretaceous age containing extinct mammals never dreamed of previously. Already he had made two or three front-page finds and the resultant publicity had raised the Cutteridge blood pressure dangerously close to the explosion stage.

Jones had not been kidding when he spoke of Indian hatchets. The Sioux were overdue for the warpath and Yavapai set as much store by his hair as anyone else but he sure wasn't honing to be sent back to Liz, dead *or* alive.

"Well," he said, as though of two minds, "it's up in the northeast end of Montana, but I ain't goin' to take no woman up there."

The professor brushed that aside. "No one asked you to."

"If you're figuring to take these wagons you'll—"

"We'll get wagons at Helena," Cutteridge decided. "Francie can dispose of the ones we've got here; the animals, too. And she can arrange for the express people to get these crates on a train for Boston. And tend to the crews we've got in the field—"

"What about *this* crew. You fixin' to fire 'em?"

"Pick out four of the best and we'll take them along. Give us a nucle—"

"You mean," Francie cried, "I'm to be left behind?"

"Well, just temporarily," her father said. "If we come onto anything important you and Harragan can join us up there."

All hands had learned when he adopted that tone there was no use arguing. "Come along," he said to Yavapai briskly. "Let's see what arrangements we can make with the railroad."

They left Salt Lake the following noon.

Cutteridge was not unheard of at Helena. Like Mainson, who had poked around in this area some months before, he was entertained by the former general, Benjamin F. Potts, presently the territorial governor of Montana. "Yes," Potts said, "there are bones in the Judith, but I don't believe I'd go up there just now. It's like I told Mainson. With these Indians moving around like they are—"

Cutteridge snorted. "All I hear anymore is Indians! If you'd make out to treat them halfway decent you wouldn't be having these scares all the time. We've killed off their buffalo, stolen their lands, broken every treaty we ever made with them, penned them like convicts—"

"I'm not responsible for federal policy," Potts said, flushing. "I've done what I could. The evil's inherent in a centralized government. It's the Boston tea party all over again. . . ."

Jones wasn't interested in politics. All he had ever got out of it was hot air, bruised knuckles and several bouts of indigestion. He knew all he wanted about Indians, though, and he thought, like the governor, that only a guy which had a few bolts loose would be fool enough to press his luck in the Judith. He had tried more than once to talk Cutteridge out of it but you might as well argue with the side of a mountain as try dissuading Daddy once he'd got his mind made up.

They traveled by coach to Fort Benton where they found folks stunned by news of the Custer massacre. Sitting Bull was said to be heading northeast and it was dollars to doughnuts he'd come straight through Benton. Half the populace had fled already, although Army units were reported on the move in an attempt to cut him off. Local opinion was not inclined to put much faith in any such likelihood. Experience with the military was seldom of a nature to inspire the recipient with any desire for a second dose. According to a Montana editorial from that era "they (the soldiers) are infrequently where one wants them and all too often where one does not."

Jones found plenty of reasons for not pressing on. Rumors put an estimated 15,000 Blackfeet, Assiniboins and Crows along the river between Benton and Fort Lincoln. Several steamboats had been fired upon.

Cutteridge, however, was much more alarmed by reports of continued Mainson discoveries. Newspaper readers, held spellbound by the appalling size of prehistoric life, were avid for details and Mainson was busily keeping them supplied with bigger and more horrendous firsts than Cutteridge so far had been able to locate.

The professor's *Nanosaurous victor*, though the only one of its kind found anywhere, because it was tiny, was lost in the scuffle. Even his contemporaries accorded it no more than passing notice so entranced were they with a sacrum vertebra described by Mainson as being more than three feet in diameter and a humerus which—he claimed—was as tall and thick as a two hundred pound man. If the Mainson diagnosis could be relied on, this predicated the prehistoric existence of a reptile seventy-eight and a half feet long!

Cutteridge, plainly, had to get back to digging.

Jones had expected—with gold placers dwindling and the ranges barred to cowmen by mass movements of Indians—to find Benton in the throes of a depression. Actually, despite all the uproar over Custer and the advance of Sitting Bull, buffalo hides were enjoying unprecedented prices and the community was booming.

Since Cutteridge insisted on continuing their journey Jones had to find horses and the only ones available were wild broncs selling for sixty-five dollars apiece, hard money. Yavapai wouldn't pay it but Cutteridge did. One concession the impatient professor reluctantly agreed to; in the interests of safety or, more probably, to speed his quest, Jones was authorized to offer one hundred dollars to every able-bodied frontiersman he could hire. After a week of miserable interviews and wrangling Jones found only five in Benton willing to risk the dangers of the trek Cutteridge contemplated.

XIII

BUT THEY got off at last and, eventually, reached the mouth of the Marias. Fording that they climbed Loma Hill, pushing eastward to come onto the Cow Island trail. By crow flight they were now less than fifty miles from their destination but the compulsions of the terrain, keeping to high ground to avoid coulee crossings, almost doubled that distance. Coming down the Buffalo Chip they debouched on the river at what became later known as the Lohse ranch and ferry but which, at the time of their foray, was inhabited only by deer, antelope, wolves and—Jones apprehensively noted—at least one band of two-legged wildlife.

It wasn't that he glimpsed either feathers or painted faces but the signs were plain to a man of his experience, and the tightened mouths of the Benton recruits amply confirmed the hidden presence. Nothing, however, was said about this, Jones himself hoping after the habit of the time that if they weren't mentioned they might go away.

Increasingly watchful the party pushed on, presently arriving at Fort Claggett, a trading post which stood at the former location of Fort Crook, abandoned in 1869.

Claggett had been established as a supply base by Mainson, and the Jones-Cutteridge group found prices considerably more inflated than those encountered at Benton, perhaps because of the added risk of trying to do business on the stamping ground of up-in-arms redmen.

While Cutteridge was there several Piegans showed up, wanting to swap horses for firearms and whisky. "Me shoot Sioux," the chief declared, suggesting he had both ears to the ground and was not above the use of a little soft soap.

Cutteridge and Jones went on up the Judith, firmly putting civilization behind them. For several days they eked out supplies with a big kill of mountain sheep. Jones had secured several extra horses equipped with pack saddles just in case they should stumble on something. The region abounded in bullberries and chokecherries.

An extended diet of sheep meat and berries Jones could make out to put up with; what really played hob with his digestive tract was the prevalence of Indians. At his best guess there must have been no less than a thousand within an hour's ride of the river. In the largest camp he counted one hundred and ten lodges, none of them Sioux but none rushing out with hugs or kisses. The feeling of constant surveillance preyed on the confidence of all but Cutteridge who pooh-poohed the idea of imminent catastrophe.

The river bottoms were thick with grazing Indian ponies. Gros Ventres were camped near Teton Creek, and they passed many parties of River Crows, Mountain Crows and the ubiquitous Piegans. All of these red men—while none offered any outright violence—were too obviously playing with matches. It was a cinch they knew of Sitting Bull's victory at the Little Big Horn, one hundred and fifty miles to the south. Every night Jones heard the whoopings and tom-toms as Crows and Blackfeet, ancient enemies, joined hands in dances of celebration.

Cutteridge continued to sleep by the fire on his pneumatic mattress while the Benton contingent, like Jones, caught what shut-eye they could in the bushes, hands clamped to rifles. Twice, Jones suggested a retreat to Fort Benton but the professor scorned the whole concept of danger. He'd fetched presents for Bear Wolf, headman of the

Crow alliance, and insisted these be delivered.

The Crow chief and Cutteridge got along as comfortably as two six-shooters thrust into the same belt. After that first visit Cutteridge told Jones, "There's no reason for nervousness. Bear Wolf told me some of his boys have just taken twenty-six scalps from the Sioux and, during recent raids, netted nine hundred horses. We're surrounded by friends."

Jones and the Bentonites, far from being at all reassured, watched uneasily as the professor, all smiles and presents, took off with a pack horse to pay a call on the Blackfoot camp. All day they sat around, morose and jumpy, wondering if Cutteridge had yet expired. Jiggs Smith, one of the Benton five, several times suggested the benefits of being long gone before the Blackfeet swooped down to count coup, but Jones' hard looks managed to hold them in line.

Cutteridge returned while they were eating a belated supper. "We got along fine," he told them. "The chief there gave me his personal assurance he's 'very big friends with all white men.'" Jones, scowling, said nothing, but before he turned in he threw a guard around the camp. When the crew assembled for breakfast, however, it was plain to be seen they were not at full strength. Four of the Benton bunch had pulled out for home. "Well, you can't hardly blame 'em," Smith said defensively, facing Jones' glower. "If that old fool keeps on the way he's going we may all be hangin' over a fire before we're done."

Some of the Bridger Basin boys appeared to think so, too, but they agreed to go on when Cutteridge finally conceded a pay hike, but the gloom of foreboding clung tenaciously to them.

With three additional pack animals obtained from the Blackfeet they headed up Dog Creek into the badlands, Jones as disgruntled as the rest of the party.

Food soon came to be in short supply but as the others began to show the result of starvation diet Cutteridge appeared more indomitable than ever. When even the pickles ran out and they were left with nothing but hardtack and bacon, and the alkali water from the creek's stony sinkholes gave the rest of them the trots, Cutteridge remained as chipper as a magpie.

It was downright disgusting, Jones felt, eying him after pulling up his pants.

September brought heavy rains to heckle

them and, during one storm, two of the horses got away and a third broke a leg and had to be shot. And, thus far, no sign at all of ancient bones had been sighted. The professor—if not discouraged—began, as his unwonted ebulliency wore thin, to exhibit indications of anxiety. "Are you certain," he asked Yavapai for the sixth or seventh time, "we are on the right trail?"

Jones wasn't certain right then of anything but did not see any need to admit it. It Mainson hadn't been over the ground he might, himself, have picked some route more abounding in game and less cluttered with breechclouts. But the tracks of wagons were too plain to be missed and all hands knew Mainson had taken two wagons up the Judith. Presently the terrain became so rough it was apparent to Jones the Philadelphian must frequently have been forced to lift and lower his vehicles by windlass. This was the Whisky Ridge country, still unmarked on modern maps.

Much of this area showed Bearpaw shale. Cutteridge several times stopped to examine tiny fossils but found no sign of the saurian remains he had been led to expect. He was beginning to eye Jones somewhat askance when a courier from Benton came up with the party near Oil Well Ridge. It wasn't called that then but that's where he found them. After making sure he was talking to Cutteridge he produced a packet of mail from his saddlebags.

Cutteridge opened the telegrams first and Jones could tell by his face the news was urgent. After reading the third he stuffed the rest of the mail in his pocket and beckoned Jones aside. "I've got to get back. It's imperative," he said. "You'll have to make out the best way you can."

Jones didn't bother to conceal his surprise. "You're givin' up the hunt?"

"I have no choice," the professor said bitterly, and chewed on his lip. "Universities!" he snarled, striding back and forth. "I've given the best years of my life to those ingrates—but do they care about that? I can thank that upstart, Mainson, for this!"

"What's the problem?" Yavapai asked as Smith drifted over, the better to hear what was graveling the management.

"Problem! I'm ordered back to explain . . . Ah, the hell with it! Just be thankful, Jones, you don't depend for your bread and butter on the whims of a set of higher learning." He resumed his pacing. "You'll have to take over."

"Right here," Smith remarked, "is where Mainson turned back."

The professor pulled up in full stride. "What's that?" he said wickedly. "How do you know?"

"Well, hell, I was with him—"

"Why didn't you say so?"

"Nobody asked me."

The old man glared. "Why'd he turn back?"

"Guess he finally decided he was wastin' his time."

The Cutteridge stare took hold of Jones fiercely. "You claimed . . . By God if you've touted me up here—You *said* there was thunder horses up in this country!"

Jones said midly, "You can't fault me on that."

Cutteridge caught Smith's grin. He began to swell up like a prodded toad. "Then why," he spluttered, half strangled, at Jones, "didn't Mainson find any?"

"Reckon," Jones said, "he didn't go far enough."

Cutteridge looked from one to the other, confused and indescribably furious. "If I thought for a minute—" He broke it off, eying Jiggs Smith's grin. "What's so funny?"

"There ain't nothin' north of here but more goddam Injuns."

"You been there?" Jones said poker-faced.

"I know fellers that has!"

"You better go back an' swap bull with 'em then. You've worn out your welcome with this expedition."

He didn't look at the professor. He knew what Cutteridge thought. Daddy wanted to believe him but was even more afraid he had been taken on a goose chase. "Buck up, Perfessor," he said, watching Smith. "I'll git them dragons out for you."

XIV

JIGGS SMITH's offer to act as guide until the scientist could be put abroad a downriver packet was brusquely accepted and the pair, forking the best two nags in Jones' caballado, took off as soon as the animals were saddled.

Nobody shed any tears at the parting.

Freeing his mind of the dozen last-minute orders he'd had no intention of obeying anyway, Yavapai loosed a hearty sigh of relief.

"Now," he said to the remaining four, "who's for card playing?"

Yips of delight signified their willingness. With the horse band hobbled close by to graze Jones produced a dog-eared deck, threw down a blanket and invited a cut. The last man to squat, hesitating uneasily, brought up a subject never far from their minds.

"Injuns? Well, I guess," Jones said, "if any comes around we can find a place for 'em. Five card draw—it's your cut, Frazier."

When the game broke up in the shank of the afternoon Jones had enriched himself by twenty-three dollars and forty-two cents, all the loose change the four could scrape up. "Looks like," he said, "this calls for a celebration." He dug out a bottle he had cached in his bedroll and they all took a swig. Driving home the cork, he grinned. "Tomorrow we git to work, boys. Them bones we been huntin' ain't a day's ride from here."

He was right. Some of the best finds Cutteridge was credited with came out of the Judith and the eight months Jones and an augmented crew spent digging around through the Bearpaw shale.

High on ridges overlain by yellow Clagget sandstone saurian fossils were discovered in large supply. Some of this sandstone was layered with bones; breakage was the biggest headache Jones faced. Too, a lot of these bones, where exposed, were too badly damaged by time and weather to be worth the trouble and expense of moving and so were abandoned.

Jones, left to himself, proved an able practical paleontologist. Cutteridge, busy back East and involved now with government and politics, made several hurried visits—with Harragan, of course, to write up their finds for posterity, but mostly Jones was left to use his own judgment.

One thing found for the first time on this continent, and excavated by Jones and his crew from the Judith Basin, was a variety of horned dinosaurs, tagged Monoclonius. The best of these, and they got every bone of it free without damage, was a fearsome creature with a horn above each eye socket and a third wickedly growing straight up out of the nasal bone. They found iguanodonts with long hind legs and tiny front ones, forebears, perhaps, of the modern kangaroo.

In the barren boulder strewn flats below the Bearpaw Mountains, Jones unearthed several hadrosaurs, a sort of kangaroo crossed with crocodile. About fifty percent of the fossils dug out of the Judith had been already discovered and identified along the Atlantic seaboard but the Montana bones assumed a grander scale; not only were these larger but in infinite variety. Some, heavily armored, were especially unique, and one group of monsters had teeth arranged in layers. A single skull held as many as 400 teeth, at least a quarter of them still in use when the reptile expired. Another creature, straight out of Burroughs, had teeth laid in like cobblestones, one side of them white, the other black.

Plainly, even with a crew running courier service, Jones wasn't able to take them all. On one of his flying trips to the diggings, Cutteridge told him: "You're going to have to pick and choose. Seems a shame—it really does—but there are hundreds of crates being stored back there now; in one room they're piled clear to the ceiling. Take at least ten years just to classify the stuff we've shipped them already. Forget about duplicates. Send back only representatives that seem truly significant."

He wiped the sweat off his glasses and took a quick look around. "I'm glad you're stacking them in separate piles." He blew out a sigh. "This business is making an old man of me—old before my time."

Jones said as he paused to wipe neck and cheeks: "I thought you enjoyed scroungin' round in—"

"It's not *bones* that bother me," the professor cried, scowling; "it's the bonehead crew the country has elected to take care of our interests back there in Washington! You would never believe men—good Christians at that—could be so corrupted! Nothing speaks loud as the almighty dollar! Jesus was right: we've got to drive the money changers out of the temple!"

The corruption that bothered and swiftly enveloped him in the snarls of red tape which were keeping him back East had been fetched to the public's attention when he'd launched a blast in the seaboard press intended to improve the sorry plight of the red man.

The particular graft which had so raised his ire was the traffic in foodstuffs, controlled at the local level—apparently—by

Indian Agents. The louder he yammered the greater the variety of persons effected, all of it done through government contract.

The successful bidder, all down the line, found himself faced with a very burdensome overhead, incurred taking care of various officials. A lot of sub-contracting was inevitably involved.

Successful bidders were bound to furnish the particular Agency (or reservation) with a prescribed tonnage of food—potatoes, meat, corn, or what have you. The most effective way contractors found of providing such subsistence and insuring a profit after paying off everyone was through lowering the quality or plain misbranding it.

Manufacturers and processors found in the system a most profitable way of emptying warehouses of unpopular items. When it came to beef—the thing, because he'd seen it, which had got the professor worked up in the first place—on top of short counts, cattle counted twice and other skulduggeries too numerous to keep track of, the animals which finally arrived for distribution were frequently so crippled or starvation poor they could scarcely stand up long enough for the kill.

With wagon freight outfits paid by the

ton, mile distances jumped to fantastic pro-portions. Everyone connected had his hand away out and, to keep him quiet, got a piece of the graft. Because it did not want its own priorities cut even the Army, fond of point-ing out the vast distances policed, inactively cooperated if only by omission. Yet the freight companies involved made mighty lit-tle out of it, being pinched in the bidding and by kickbacks spread clean across the prairie. One way they discovered to help offset this was by swapping salable sundries from their Indian manifests to unscrupulous storekeepers for bulged canned goods, spoiled flour and cornmeal enough to make the right weight.

Not satisfied with his blasts in the papers, Cutteridge had personally gone straight to Washington and presented himself to Col-ombus Delano, in charge of Indian affairs as Grant's Secretary of the Interior. When the Secretary refused to see him Cutteridge carried his outrage to Grant. The President saw him.

The professor's fireworks in the press had put the whole kettle of fish right onto the front pages. The papers sent delegates to call on Delano. Naturally alarmed, Delano, in fear and wrath, was precipated into statements a cooler mind must have regretted. Cutteridge, he cried, was trying to pamper the Indians, interfering with the benevolent Department policy by which these government charges were rapidly becoming not only provident farmers but "industrious tillers of the soil." Professors and busybodies inevitably, he suggested, did nothing but stir up tempests in teapots. Cutteridge obviously was a case in point, undermining public confidence, hoodwinked into going off half-cocked. The Indians were being well looked after, their best interests ever his first consideration.

Cutteridge, answering with another salvo, was called by Delano a "mugwamp," Democrat, a Confederate lover, and a "plain preposterous downright liar." Furthermore, the Secretary implied, Cutteridge—openly an enemy of morals and religion—should be looked into for subversive activities, corrupting the country's youth by making the Bible out to be a lie with the crews he had digging up the West to prove everyone had evolved from apes.

The professor called Delano most of the things generally reserved for Mainson and repeated his charges over and over. Grant, with reason, was understandably upset. A great admirer of wealth and prominence, he could hardly fail to be aware that Cutteridge, almost continuously in the papers, could be a fearsome antagonist, a man with entrée into circles of culture which would have shut their doors in Delano's face.

He tried his best to "hush up the furor" and, when this didn't work, he was finally forced to fire somebody. This did not noticeably help the Indians but it did boost Cutteridge's stock no end. Its lingering memory continued to open doors for him throughout the entire balance of his career. Flushed with this victory he was ready now, he confided in Jones, to show Mainson up for the charlatan he was.

XV

BUT MAINSON had quite a lot of things going for him, not the least of which was personal charm. He could talk a widow straight out of her skirt or anything else she was like to set store by. He could appropriate the credit for other folks' finds and yet they'd still go out of their way to fetch him other discoveries—even proselyte friends and far-off aquaintances. He kept from eight to ten crews in the field the year round. The reporters liked him and he was prodigal with money.

These were advantages Cutteridge did not have. The professor's chip-on-shoulder disposition won few friends and made new enemies everywhere he went. Except for Harragan—who had the inside track—the press considered him a pompous, silver-plated S.O.B. But he made good copy and, for that reason, got at least twice the coverage accorded his rival save in and about Ernest Henry's home town.

Cutteridge had the university back of him, the learned societies and his philanthropist uncle's name and prestige. He was more painstaking, less likely to gamble than the coal king's son. He was, perhaps, better versed, in his own field a perfectionist, though no more above pilfering and plundering than the man he called an unscrupulous upstart.

A man in Colorado, an Oxford graduate named Jason Dykes, found the vertebra of a truly huge animal on a shale strewn ridge near Morrison. Continued search in the heat of his excitement produced other finds of academic interest, among these a femur fourteen inches across the base and fully as tall as Dykes himself.

He took his discoveries and stored them in town in a borrowed shed which he fitted with a padlock. Sending word to Cutteridge, he hustled back to his ridge and, in due course, dug up a ton of outsized prehistoric fossils. Though the professor had not answered, thinking perhaps the proof might move him Dykes crated up the best of his finds and put them on a train for Boston. Hooked with the bug he went back to his digging and several weeks later, still with no word from Cutteridge, consigned his next load of fossils to Mainson in Philadelphia.

The professor, with Jones and three other crews digging like mad, had boxes coming in three or four times a week and hadn't got around to examining Dykes' bones. Mail had stacked up till he despaired of ever answering it. One thing, though, that he did keep an eye on was Mainson's credits and, when the Philadelphia began publishing reports of his Colorado discoveries, Cutteridge remembered the letter from Morrison, found it, read it, opened the crates and feverishly got off a telegram to Dykes: HAVE

NO MORE DEALINGS WITH MAINSON STOP FUR-
THER COMMUNICATIONS FOLLOW.

But the telegram was never delivered. Dykes, of course, was off hunting fossils. When four days went by without reply, the professor got on a hot line to Jones, explained the situation, told him to get over to Morrison right away and purchase title to the fossils sent Mainson.

As a master persuader Yavapai may have lacked the polished approach and engaging charm of Ernest Henry Mainson but he was not without resource and, after tracking Dykes to the bone quarry, sent Cutteridge title to the fossils Mainson, with such fanfare, had been exploiting in the press.

When caught in a tight spot Ernest Henry was adept at extricating himself without discernible loss of face. Passing it off with a good-natured laugh, obviously the victim of a misunderstanding, he relinquished at least a portion of Dykes' shipment, the part he had publicly identified and which was already credited to him anyway.

Actually he was after bigger fish just then. At about the time Dykes found his first bones another Colorado pundit, Superintendent of Schools for Fremont County, had unearthed similar relics outside Canon City at a place called Garden Park. This gentle-man, too, had first approached Cutteridge and been turned over to one of his aides, a vertebrate paleontologist named Joshua Keyes. While Keyes was attempting to ne-gotiate the tract Mainson, with the quiet of a spider, was buying up the Superinten-dent's claim to Garden Park.

Cutteridge was back in Boston when ru-mors of the Garden Park fossils chanced to catch up with him. Straws in the wind, nothing definite at all, but the professor wired Keyes to go down and mosey around. In the guise of representative of a pickle manufacturer Keyes appeared on the scene incognito. The town was filled with strangers. First thing Keyes discovered was the articulated skeleton of a baby dinosaur, scarcely larger than a wolf, peering out at him from a gift shop window.

He telegraphed Cutteridge. SECURE ALL BONES POSSIBLE, the professor wired back. MAINSON VIOLATING ALL AGREEMENTS.

Keyes purchased the miniature skeleton for three dollars and shipped it forthwith to his employer in Boston. But Mainson, he discovered, was already hauling some pretty fantastic specimens from the hole being opened at Garden Park, nine miles northeast of Canon City. These bones were running considerably larger than the fossils Jones was getting from the Morrison diggings.

Suddenly the paper were filled with Mainson fanfare telling the marvels of the fantastic colossus dubbed *Diplodocus* which his Garden Park crew were just now uncovering.

Cutteridge got off the train at Canon City with blood in his eye. He had Jones with him, Yavapai wearing his big hat and six-shooter and looking like a marshal straight out of Fort Smith. Sight of their stern faces brought them with a minimum of chin music to the Superintendent's sanctum. Cutteridge, coming at once to the point, demanded to be shown the contract the Colorado educator had signed with Ernest Henry.

With the document scarcely unfolded—Jones peering over his shoulder—Cutteridge cried: "You've been robbed! Do you realize, sir, you've sold out the paleontological find of the century for what amounts to a sorry pittance? I'd have paid you three times that—and gladly!"

Jones, with guileful cunning, put in to say that all was possibly not yet lost. This agreement, obviously consummated under false pretenses, could hardly be worth the paper it was written on. Even taken at face value, he pointed out, what their rival had purchased was not the actual quarry but only the "remainder of the fossils." "Hell, it says so right there!" he said, putting a thumb on it.

The professor nodded. "We can see that much. What are you getting at?"

"Well, if Mainson's bought only such bones as will complete the skeletons he's already got parts of, the Super here's certainly the owner of anything not already turned up."

Cutteridge, as though this had not occured to him, clapped one hand to his brow and clucked. "I'd be willing," he mentioned after thinking a minute, "to pay quite a price to take over what's left. . . ."

The Superintendent appeared to be somewhat dubious about the ethics of such a proposal but with Jones' hard looks and the paraded artillery that swung at his hip the professor managed to force payment on him. Jones, hard bargainer, insisted they be given a paper recording the transaction— "Somebody's got to look after the rights of this business."

The paper extracted and folded away, Jones and his boss moved out to the diggings. Cutteridge now had title to the quarry but a larger headache swiftly loomed when it came to deciding which bones belonged to what. Ernest Henry with some words about claim jumping solved the problem by refusing to recognize that Cutteridge had any rights at all. Already dug in and substantially backed by the group of armed malcontents he'd recruited from up around Central City, he invited the professor, and Jones in particular, to start making tracks.

Jones peered at Cutteridge. The professor glared back. Jones assayed the scowls, added them to the rifles, folded the lips over his teeth and set off down the hill. Cutteridge, snarling abuse, tramped after him.

XVI

CUTTERIDGE, FURIOUS, sent for Harragan. Francie came with him but, even with her to flatter and inspire him, the *Transcript*'s man—despite a flood of scurrilous stories —was unable to dislodge Ernest Henry from the Garden Peak diggings.

After three weeks of this windy squabble

during which the term "claim jumper" was freely flung from camp to camp, Mainson succeeded in signing another contract with the Superintendent and, thus armed with two bills of sale, had an obvious advantage should Cutteridge seek redress from the courts.

Jones said, "Hell, there's bound to be other bones around here someplace," and hiring a crew he set out to find them.

With the experience gained from his three years with Cutteridge he soon uncovered a dig not far off, found the owner of the land and clinched their rights with a twelve-months lease. The professor had gone grumbling off to Kansas when Jones, supervising the diggers, stumbled over a bit of rusty looking rock which, surreptitiously, he'd thrust in a pocket. Harragan had left with Cutteridge but Francie had elected to stay on the job, for both she and Daddy had seen pretty clearly that without someone kept a consistently close eye on Jones he might well do something crazy. Like haring off after that hasher-turned-warbler.

When the bones started piling up to be readied for shipment Francie gave Jones a raise and, by way of celebration, even took him to town. He'd done his level best to play up but his attention kept wandering. This new dig, too, was rather disappointing. The whole country was in the throes of a depression and, while the new site yielded an abundance of bones, the fossils were bedded in very hard sandstone and more were broken getting them out than were put aside for crating. The best they found had already been discovered and identified by Ernest Henry.

After several weeks of duplicating Mainson's Garden Park finds Jones began rather noticeably to reveal indications of wanting to pull out. That girl from Redskin appeared to have dealt him a deeper hurt than a reasonable person would have thought possible. It was the first time Francie had encountered such indifference to discrete displays of her voluptuous charms.

Her chin took a firmer line. She treated herself to a whole new wardrobe—real provocative stuff, and tried leading him on. He did not even seem to notice the bait. For one so amply endowed as Francie such a lack of interest was pretty vexatious. It just had to stem from another woman, and who could there be but that Redskin hash house keeper's horse-faced daughter!

To even imagine such a state of affairs

was almost more than Miss Cutteridge could stomach. She plopped herself down in front of a mirror and, seething, took stock of her flushed reflection without turning up any sign of a flaw. Yet preposterous as she knew it to be she felt resentfully certain it was that lantern jawed Hester that had turned Jones into a walking zombi.

What to do about it was not so easily arrived at. She guessed Daddy's influence could probably encompass black-listing her rival from the music hall circuit, but this would likely drive her back to the only address Jones had for her finding her—and, besides, it would be an admission of defeat, a thing she found too painful to contemplate.

It wasn't as though she'd any use for Jones personally. She would not wipe her feet on the fellow! But she had to know she *could* if she wanted to. Daddy needed him. And he was no good to Daddy stumbling around on the job like a moonstruck calf!

Things rocked along for a couple of weeks with Jones still looking like he'd lost some of his marbles and Francie, still smarting, leaving no stone unturned which might— even temporarily—free Daddy's field boss from the albatross that biscuit-shooting warbler had hung around his neck. Searching back through the papers which came almost daily with the mountain of mail passed on to her from Boston she found them filled with stories of Mainson's discoveries with only an occasional brief mention of Daddy, and never anywhere near the coveted front pages.

The plight of the Cutteridge stock looked desperate. Someway Jones had to be got back to work or they might find themselves right out in the street! Not even Daddy's uncle or that wonderful museum would be able to save his chair for long if Jones didn't make another big find quick!

On a gloomy Saturday under overcast skies she stumbled onto a wallet near a stack of fossils set aside for crating. A grimy looking thing with bent-over corners, the sweat darkened leather scarred and battered from long usage, one of those hand-crafted Mexican items so prevalent now in the curio shops.

She picked it up gingerly, distastefully opening it, mostly to see if she could find who it belonged to. It was bulging with banknotes and, when she removed these to count them, a tiny tintype fell out. Stopping to retrieve it she went as suddenly rigid as though she'd picked up a snake. It was Hester's pictured likeness, big mouth as smugly smiling as a cat standing over a flutter of feathers.

Francie flung the hateful thing to the ground, and the wallet after it, banknotes and all. Serve him right if somebody stole it! A man too irresponsible even to take care of his own money! Out of spite she kicked it under the bones. Let him hunt for it, curse him! At least it would take his fool mind off that strumpet!

But apparently he didn't even know it was missing. On Monday, relenting, she fished it out and, calling him over to her tent, gave it to him with a few potent thoughts on taking care of his property. Most of which, obviously, went in one ear and out the other as, thumbing through that wad of bills, with a deepening scowl he all but turned the thing inside out.

No one had to tell Francie what he was looking for. "Oh, go on," she cried, exasperated—"get out!"

These were the great days of railroad expansion. All over the boondocks—at uncounted hundreds of water tanks and flag stops—a never-surveyed number of red-blooded young fellows in black sleeve protectors and green eyeshades crouched in lonely vigil above a clacking brass key completely forgotten by the world at large.

With nothing to stare at but rails running off into shimmering infinity through the flora and fauna of the thousand empty miles, unless one counted an occasional line-riding cowpoke stopping by for company, it might seem an astonishing wonder the whole kit and caboodle didn't end up wacky as sheepherders.

But that was in a time when Americans didn't have the dole to fall back on, before the government paid bonuses to unwed mothers and most of the monkeys were kept in a zoo. Young fellows of that era had a backbone to lean on, a belief that idle hands were apt for the devil's employment. They found better ways of whiling away the endless hours at their masterless posts than propping up hell to slip a chunk under it.

More than a few succeeded in taming local wildlife—one enterprising youngster is reputed to have taught his pet rattlesnake to read Morse code. The story is told how the agent at Buckley learned to shed his skin and had the result of one of these molting periods mounted by a taxidermist and put on display at a famous world's fair. At Como, Wyoming, a telegrapher discovered what eventually amounted to the greatest horde of reptile bones ever dug out of the American West.

Como, being hardly more than a flag stop in those days, boasted a population of twenty-five. Nobody said whether these were people, but the only human you'd be likely to find was the brass key man, Charlie Finter, marooned in that station and seldom remembered except once a month by the company's bookkeeper and the railroad official who put his John Henry upon Finter's checks.

Occasionally punchers from the Medicine Bow country would stop off for a bit to shoot the breeze while waiting for the up or down train to scream past. Most of this tribe had got into the habit of grazing their ponies on grounded reins, but one or two specimens refused to stay put and, rather than go to the bother of hunting them, the owners of such nags commonly attached them to what was known as "a drag." The Como drag appeared to be a fairly substantial cottonwood burl; but one day, having nothing better to do, Finter—who'd become an inveterate reader of whatever newspapers got tossed off with the infrequent mail—chancing to examine it, let out a whistle of excited astonishment.

It was a bone, and dang peculiar.

"Hell," he said to himself—a picked-up habit he was somewhat ashamed of, "maybe it's one of them dinosaur bones!" And he couldn't have come closer if he'd used an express rider's sawed-off Greener. The burl, several months later, on expert opinion, turned out to be the tail weapon of a *Stregosaurus*, a fantastic prehistoric reptile with fabulous armored back fins, practically no head and a tail it used after the fashion of a club in the hands of a berserk caveman.

Speculating about it, Finter looked around between trains in the hope of finding other fossils. Luck was with him. Up the track a few hundred yards where debris from shaving the side of a bluff had firmed a bed for the gandy dancers he opened up a drift and found more fossils.

Finter was no fool. He was up Darwin and the missing link hunters. Engrossed by exaggerated rumors of prices paid for bits and pieces of things like this he put every spare minute into deepening the hole. The prospect triggered by boredom attained astonishing impetus from roseate visions of wealth and fame.

Evenings when it was too dark to dig without exposing his hand by lamp or candle he spent on the station platform trying to dredge from memory the name of that paleontologist from Boston. It was Mainson who flung around money so reckless but in Finter's thoughts the professor bulked largest.

He'd given his last paper to one of them cowpokes and the next ten thrown off were filled with the exploits of Ernest Henry and the Garden Park discoveries. Finter stubbornly clung to the erroneous notion that feller from Boston was the one to do business with. The pile of bones grew and one morning, pausing to sleeve the sweat from his eyes, the name came to him.

Dashing back to his station he was all set to send off a wire when some sixth sense of caution momentarily restrained him. This job didn't look to have a hell of a lot of future but in these lean times at least it meant eating. He could not believe his penny-pinching bosses would consider at all kindly this dig he had embarked on. He got a sun-yellowed envelope out of his desk and stepped over to the Oliver. By the hunt and peck system he typed "C.C. CUTTE-RIDGE, PROFESSOR OF PALENTOLOGY, BOSTON, MASS."

He tore a sheet of cerise lined paper off a pad and resolutely rolled it into the machine. Then he sat a while thinking and, to the best of his ability, typed a description of the bones he'd uncovered. After which with a brooding frown he apprehensively considered the wrath to come should his employers happen to catch wind of this exploit. To be on the safe side he signed a fictitious name.

What the hell. Any mail dumped off he would have first look at. Reassured by this notion he put his letter on the next eastbound train.

XVII

SINCE THE mixup over that skull which had allowed Ernest Henry to get the jump on Calaveras Man the professor had instructed his Boston office that hereinafter when he wasn't available all incoming wires and first class mail should be readdressed and promptly forwarded to Francie and thus, in due course, she opened Finter's letter.

Normally she might not have paid much attention; people were always writing Daddy about bones they wanted classified or the marvelous finds some friend had dug up and wouldn't he like to have first crack at them? Most of this was rubbish, but mail of late had been running largely to duns and promotional matter as a result of Cutteridge's absence from the nation's front pages. Also the university was becoming acidulously importunate and Francie saw in the Como query a means of channeling Yavapai's dissipated energies into something more possible of profit to Daddy than his carryings-on for the past month had been. Anything, she thought, to get his mind out of the bottle and off that mining camp hasher turned music hall tart!

Armed with her father's power of attorney she sent off a check and covering letter to Thaddeus Carp. Then she called in Jones and told him they were catching the next train to Laramie.

"Laramie!" he hooted. "What's to go up there fer? You goin' in fer belted earls or some of them remittance men?"

She handed him Finter's letter.

"Como, fer God's sake!" He looked up, scowling. "Never heard of the burg!" He

135

poked his head outside to yell at one of the crew, a recent blond pick-up who called himself Cheyenne. Hauling his head back Jones said sourly, "At least you got the right direction; it's on the Northern Pacific west of Medicine Bow." He said with sweeping contempt: "Nothin' up there. Just be wastin' our time."

"You've wasted enough around here. Get your things packed."

Jones said flatly that he wasn't going.

The Cutteridge chin began to show through her patience.

"You want to go back to fishing cigar butts out of cuspidors?"

It was a question figured to put Jones in his place and if it did not kick all the ringiness out of him it certainly took most of the wind from his sails.

"I've had enough of your tantrums," she told him bluntly. "You were hired to find bones and it's time you got at it." She lifted the phone and called the Canon City depot. "An obligation, Jones, is a state of being indebted. When you let my father bail you out of that saloon—"

"Well, Jesus Christ," Jones yelled in a fury, "I didn't hire out to bind myself to him *forever!*"

"Is this the Canon City depot?" she said into the phone. "I wonder if you could tell me where in Wyoming the town of Como is located? There isn't . . . Oh, I see. How soon could you get me booked through?—This is Francine Cutteridge. It's important that I get there at the earliest convenience. . . . Mmmm . . . If that's the best you can do—Yes. I'll want two tickets. Just the one way."

She hung up, still watching Jones. "It's on the N. P., a flag stop south of Medicine Bow. We'll have to make several changes. The best we can get is day coaches but we leave Canon City tonight. And"—like grappling hooks her eyes took hold of him—"if you're dredging up some way that you can maybe duck out of this, just stop and think a minute about what Daddy got you out of. You might get away from me but the Pinkertons will find you, and that hasher won't be round to kiss your tears away. Believe me."

What with changing trains and layovers it took them two nights and the best part of three days to find the place Carp's letter had come from and neither of the cowpunchers goggling at Francie had ever heard tell of anyone going by such an outlandish name. After one look around, Jones, still surly-eyed, followed the sound of the telegraph key into the station for his first look at Finter.

"Just a second," Charlie said, frantically scribbling on a yellow sheet of paper. Dropping his stub of pencil he hurried outside and, with a startled look at Francie standing by their luggage the cynosure of all eyes, he jumped to the track, threw a switch and, peering disgusted at the open-mouthed punchers said, touching his eyeshade, "Anything I can do for you, Miss?"

"Where's the town?" she asked, showing him her teeth.

"Yeah," he grinned back, "ain't that something? Eighteen months I been stuck with this key and haven't seen hide nor hair of it yet."

"Have you seen any bones?" Francie shot back, and his jaw flopped down like a blacksmith's apron.

With a nervous scowl at the two representatives of vested interests he got hold of himself enough to say, herding her away from them, "Better come inside, Miss, out of this heat. Your bags'll be all right where they're at." To the cowboys with another hard look he said with a kind of testy assurance, "That wall can make out to stand without help from the Quarter Circle G in case you got business someplace else," and slammed the door shut behind them.

Jones was staring at a slip of pink paper propped against an inkwell back of Finter's key. Charlie was about to ask Francie what kind of bones she had in mind when, flushing, he caught up the check some scant three inches ahead of Jones' reach. Francie said, "Is that yours?"

Finter looked like a caught fence crawler.

"I'm Francine Cutteridge," she told him, smiling, and the sweating agent heaved a sigh of relief.

"Am I glad to see *you!* Couldn't cash the dang—my name's Finter. Charlie Finter—"

"What are you doin' with Thaddeus Carp's check?" That was Jones, and the sound of his voice roughly matched the look coming out of that scrinched-up pale blue stare.

The flush on Finter's harassed face spread down into the open collar of his shirt. He appealed to Francie. "You *did* say your name was Cutteridge, didn't you?"

Francie nodded. "I signed that check."

"This feller ain't connected with the

139

N.P., is he?" Finter asked, eying Jones from the corner of his stare.

Francie laughed. "So that's why you signed 'Thaddeus Carp' to your letter. You were afraid you might get into trouble with the railroad."

"Well," Finter said, "it's a job. I guess. Thought it would be better not to put my own name on it."

"Then you did find some bones?"

"Lordy—yes! Got a whole passle of 'em crated behind the station."

"Let's have a look at them," Francie said, all business. "Oh—" She flashed a look at Jones. "This is Yavapai Jones. He's in charge of our diggers."

Jones grunted sourly. "Horse bones most likely." But he tagged along.

The crate when they got to it was about five by three by three and a half. How this local yokel had figured to move it short of a crane Jones couldn't guess, but his look turned more lively when Finter pinch-barred a board off. "Well," he said, squinting, "you just might of found somethin'. Where at's the hole?"

"Come on," Finter said, and off they went.

XVIII

UNBEKNOWNST TO our friends, Mainson, who had spies everywhere, had not been completely caught with his pants down. At about the time Finter's letter, rerouted, had begun the trek West on its hunt for Francie, another—from Cutteridge's Boston office —had been dispatched post haste to Ernest Henry at Garden Park. While he was tearing this open someone at the Canon City depot sent a boy on a fast horse hustling to the scene of his labors with word of Miss Cutteridge's interest in Como.

It did not take Ernest Henry long to put these two things together and come up with the notion a trip to Wyoming might be just what the doctor ordered. Accordingly, suitably accompanied, he boarded the next train out of Colorado, scarcely twelve hours behind the one carrying Jones.

But Jones, once he'd seen what Finter had to offer, settled into his collar like an old fire horse and for the rest of that day things hummed around Como. With Francie's connivance he hired the two ranch hands, at big pay and the further temptation of a prodigal bonus, away from their allegiance to the Quarter Circle G. In midafternoon a rider drifting west from Medicine Bow was put on the payroll at extravagant wages and Finter, flushed with excitement and proximity to Francie, was put to work sending wires to Cutteridge in Washington and the crew Jones had left in Colorado. And, when this was done and the Como fossils securely sewn up with an ironclad contract, Jones got him busy on a series of two-by-four signs which said in black paint at least three inches wide WARNING—NO TRESPASS.

When Mainson & Company got off the train at Como next morning they were met at the bluff by three hardfaced rifle packers standing back of the signs, and it was almighty plain that these fellows meant business.

Jones waved sardonically and, coming up to them, said: "You can squat on your carpetbags right there in the sun till the eastbound gits here. When it leaves you better be on it."

Mainson looked at him pleasantly. Then, with a whimsical glance at his companions: "Well, you can't win them all, gentlemen," and brought his regard back to Yavapai.

"Jones," he said, "how'd you like to be counted among the victors for a change?"

Jones let out a guffaw.

If highrolling Henry was offended he hid it well; he even chuckled a little with a reasonable man's appreciation of this unexpected reversal. Then he brushed it away. "Skirmishes never win a war," he smiled. "It's the long haul that counts. You've only to look through the past two months' papers to find the name of the man who'll go down in history as the greatest paleontologist America produced. What you hear is Opportunity knocking. Better climb on the wagon."

The two men with him had not so far opened their mouths but Jones could tell from their looks they were a couple of college bred scientists; and he'd been wanting ever since that brush-off from Hester away back at Salt Lake to sever a connection grown daily more odious.

"I'm quite serious, Jones," Ernest Henry assured him. "You're too good a man to go down with the ship. I'll pay you three times what you're getting from Cutty and every new thing you turn up will fetch a bonus."

Francie, hearing voices, came hurrying out of Finter's prospect and, with her flying toward him, Jones was mightily tempted. "I guess not," he said finally, folding his arms. "To hard fer an ol' dog to learn new tricks." Then, for Francie's benefit, "Thanks just the same."

She considered him blankly; then more sharply, suspicious, swiveled her black stare at Mainson. "What do you four-flushers think you're doing here?"

Mainson turned on his charm. "I've been offering your straw boss a job on my staff," he said unabashed, with a bright flash of teeth. "One can see now why he's reluctant to change."

"Flattery will get you noplace." She scowled. "I can't see how you got onto this so quick."

"Well," Mainson chuckled, "we all have our sources. It's been nice," he said, "seeing you again, Miss Cutteridge," and lifted his bowler, turning grandly away.

"Here—wait!" she called as he moved toward the station.

"They're not going noplace till that train comes along." In a swivel of light Jones whipped out his pistol. Two reports fanned out. The lap and rattle of churned-up grit fell off Mainson's shoes and the fronts of his pantslegs.

Having blown the smoke from the barrel of his weapon Yavapai—a real fast learner—displayed a fair imitation of the Mainson lifted lip. "They're not about to git anywheres near that depot. Fer this transaction one bill o' sale's aplenty. They can git their tickets when they climb aboard."

Francie may not have caught the full gist but it was clear Mainson had.

Through a tight glint of teeth his breath came harshly but he wasn't a man to let temper color his judgement. "When you're tired," he said, "of strewing pearls before swine a call put through Philadelphia will reach me."

Breasts brushing against him, Francie took hold of Jones' arm like a wife. "It will be forty below on the porch of the hot place when you collect any calls from this camp!"

If the Philadelphian's smile was skeptical he knew when to leave well enough alone.

Jones' crew arrived at Como with the equipment he had sent for and the bluff became a beehive of almost around-the-clock activity. Cutteridge came a few days later with his man-on-loan from the Boston *Transcript* and, for as long as he stayed, there was never an idle moment for anyone.

Their first big find was *Atlantosaurus*,

sixty feet long and as fearsome looking as a spinster's nightmare—Harragan saw that the wires were kept open straight through to Bean Town. Next came a mammoth reptilian monster with terrible claws and teeth like ax heads; Francie named this one *Allosaurus*, and Cutteridge was back in the news with a bang. Then, after a couple of carloads of fossils that only duplicated finds made earlier elsewhere, Jones' augmented army of diggers uncovered *Brontosaurus excelsus* that made the front pages from coast to coast and even was heralded by no less a paper than the *London Times*. This was a saurus every one of whose paw prints measured a square yard across and whose articulated skeleton was enough to make one swear off drinking.

Cutteridge, now at the peak of his career, looked in good shape to eclipse every claim to fame made by his Philadelphia rival whose prestige had recently soared like a rocket, only to fall before Daddy's triumphs just about as unnoticed as the rocket's stick.

Leaving Harragan behind to keep the wires humming, Cutty departed on a tour that packed every hall he could be persuaded to appear in. It was after he left that one of Jones' scouts, off with pack horses to find meat for the pot, stumbled out in the wilds on a cabin built entirely of dinosaur bones. Some sheepherder's shack, apparently abandoned.

Francie was delighted—even Yavapai showed an unexpected excitement when he declared with cowpuncher aptness, "We'll call it Bone Cabin!" and peered around at Francie from the corners of his eyes. "I'll take three of the boys—includin' Jim here, an' git right over there straightaway."

"I'll go with you," Francie said, catching hold of him. But Jones—not always at his best with her hovering over him—said, quick thinking: "Hi gollies! Who's to tend store with the both of us gone? You go ahead, Francie; I'll look when you git back. Ain't likely," he decided with a thoughtful frown, "Mainson—if he's snooping' round —would go so far as t' shoot a lady."

Francie, all set to join a laugh, looked a bit nonplussed when she didn't hear any. "You don't honestly think . . . ?"

Jones, mighty serious, shook his head. "Hard to say *what* a feller like that, backed out of the limelight like he's been by your dad . . . One thing's sure as God grows little apples! He's a sight too slick not to've been keepin' cases. One of us better git right on over there. This Como dig won't last forever and if we don't stake that Bone Cabin country—"

"I hadn't thought about that," Francie said, looking worried.

Jones' scout spoke up. "Was a time there—Saturday, before I happened onto that cabin—I'd of swore, by godfries, there was somebody doggin' my tracks sure as Sunday."

"You catch a look at 'em?" Jones said, scrinching his eyes up.

"Funny thing about that," the meat hunter grumbled. "Doubled back, I did, three-four times. Never located so much as a footprint, never saw nobody, never heard a sound. But I'd swear there was eyes on me half the mornin'."

"You go ahead," Francie said, taking her hold off him to tuck in stray wisps of her golden hair. "I'd better be seeing about crates for these fossils, and . . ." The rest trailed away while she stared at him searchingly. "Do you suppose it was *Indians?*"

"It could be, ma'am," Jim said; and Jones, tapping his six-shooter, grunted, "They'll be damn dead Injuns, they come foolin' round me!" He turned to the meat man. "You go round up Joe an' Charlie,

Jim, an' we'll hit on over there straightaway. You tell them boys to fetch their Winchesters."

XIX

IT OCCURED to Jones if there *was* anyone creeping around through the brush it was a heap more likely to have been Shoshones than somebody trying to play spy for Ernest Henry. He wasn't particularly worried about it but, like the other three, kept one eye peeled and a hand within easy reach of his rifle. Nor was he very much interested, right at this moment, in the fossil possibilities of this place they were headed for.

What he did have in mind was the same bright notion which had hatched when Jim had come busting in with news of this find. That here was his chance to slip away for a bit, to go over the hump and—with any luck at all—to maybe cut loose of the whole Cutteridge tribe—big Daddy included.

He had the experience now to hunt these critters on his own and a roll in his pocket that, if it might not choke a cow, was of sufficient weight and substance it should go a long way toward patching things up. She was a good girl—Hester. A real hard worker with her feet on the ground.

He guessed he should have seen all this back at Redskin instead of letting himself be dazzled by a pile of gab and a well turned ankle. Just to brush against the subject made him squirm in his clothes for knowing right well that wasn't the whole of it. Made him blush and growl every time he put his mind to it. The rock-bottom truth was what had made a fool of him was the button-popping look at little yellow-haired Francie crammed into them slinky damn five dollar shirts!

But he was onto her now. He had his eyes wide open. The only one Francie cared two hoots about was Francie herself and what happened to Daddy! She'd never cared about him—he'd been just a convenience, same as pouty-cheeked Harragan and all them others who'd been dumb enough to let her husky-voiced whoppers send them flying through tossed hoops.

Women could do them kind of things to a man. It was enough to cramp rats the way some women could put a guy through the wringer—he thanked the good Lord he had come to his senses, could only hug the hope it hadn't been too late.

A feller never knew his luck. Back there at Redskin he'd had the world by the tail. He forgot about Liz and the jeers of the merchants. He had never—he remembered now—had things so good. A going business to fall into, free drinks, free meals and a hard working woman who'd thought the sun rose and set in him.

And he had thrown it all over to go loping after that come-hither Francie with her bouncing boobs and a calculation colder than a bartender's heart!

"By Gawd I ort t' be bored fer the simples!"

"What's that?" Jim asked, twisting around in his saddle.

Yavapai scowled. "You tend t' your knittin'." When a guy started talking out loud to himself he wasn't far from being ready to drag around a string of spools! Irritably he said, "How much farther to this goddam cabin?"

The hunter peered at him astonished. "Even pushin' these nags we couldn't git there 'fore t'morrer. I kinder figgered about noon."

"Mebbe," Jones said, scowling, "be a good idea if I was to kind of drift off ahead fer a—"

"Ahead of what?" Jim asked, looking considerably suspicious. "If you don't know where that cabin's at . . ." The Saint Bernard wrinkles puckered deeper around his stare. "You wouldn't be thinkin' now to git yourself lost, would you?"

Jones let out a gravelly snort, but if his restive thoughts continued to pick at it he was careful not to call attention to the fact. When a man got ready to roll his cotton he'd better figure to make some pretty far apart tracks. A guy could look pretty foolish getting hauled back to listen to Francie's views on the subject.

They rode well into the deepening twilight and made a dry camp among the rocks of a knoll that overlooked considerable country. While none of them were really too concerned about Indians this meat hunter, Jim, showed himself a careful man. Jones didn't think the feller was taking double pay but there wasn't much doubt he intended to sleep with one eye open.

Two different times, Jones, preparing to slip from his blankets, found Jim propped on an elbow watching him. "Stone gougin' your hip?" the hunter, on the second occasion, asked with a sardonic edge to his voice. "You seem t' be havin' a hard time restin'."

"Thought I heard somethin'," Jones whispered back, twisting his head to peer around through the dark; and Jim, playing up to it, all too obligingly, threw back his soogans. "I'll take a look."

Jones saw the Winchester in his hands when he stood up to drift from sight on spurless boots.

Wasn't much chance getting away from here now, he thought, disgusted. Thinking back in the light of this palpable suspicion he recalled, just before they'd took off from Como, seeing Francie and this jigger mighty close in conversation. So maybe he was being paid to make sure doubly certain there didn't nobody get lost or parted from this pasear.

Yavapai, fuming, settled into his blankets, feeling too mean to get any proper rest. But sometime in the smaller hours he must eventually have drowsed because the next thing he knew the night was filled with the wildest yells any man would want to hear this side of Jordan. He jumped up, swearing, scrabbling around for his rifle as a rocket of stampeding hooves swept past with muzzle lights winking and guns going off all over the place.

This was Injuns, all right—no one had to tell Jones that, nor why them devils had come swarming over them. Listening to the receding sounds of their travel told him plain enough this breech-clout coup had been a heap more successful than was going to bear much thinking of. In *his* mind at least it was a foregone conclusion those goddam Shosones had got away with most if not all of their horses.

"Think they'll be back?" somebody called out, nervous.

Jones ripped out an oath. "Why the hell would they? They got what they come fer!"

The other crew member, Joe Bandle, said shivery as frog's legs, "I figgered, by Gawd, they was here t'lift hair!"

"They know we won't git far on shanks' mare," Jones grumbled, and looked around bitterly as someone struck a light.

Only one he didn't see was that meat-hunting Jim. Determined to keep the boss immobilized Jim would have stashed himself out where he could keep a peeled eye on the picket roped remuda. Them red devils would have tended to him first thing.

And they had.

He wouldn't ever, Yavapai saw, peering down at what they'd left, be any deader.

XX

NEAR AS he could make out there were just two choices, neither of them what you might call real encouraging. They could push on, hoping to locate that cabin, or they could make a stab at getting back to Como where they could pick up more hands and a fresh string of ponies. Either way the possibilities for survival could not help but seem mighty slim.

Of course it all depended on whether them Injuns had been after horses or wanted something else. Jones had been around redskins enough to believe no one but a nump who didn't have all his marbles would attempt to apply logic to anything they did.

A lot of guys trapped in his kind of dilemma might have put it to a vote, thus absolving themselves of all responsibility. Jones scarcely gave this a second thought. You might think they'd have a better chance if they all stuck together, but with his own wants strong in mind he wasn't about to insist on anything.

"Them Shooshonnies," he told them, "will likely expect us to heat up the back-trail—it's what whites generally do caught in a bind. I don't know where this Bone Cabin's at but I'm goin' to look fer it. You fellers can do whatever best suits you."

"Man, you crazy?" Bandle gaped.

Yavapai shrugged. He didn't even bother to hunt up saddle or blankets. He divided the grub into three equal shares, started stuffing his pockets. He would have more fire power if they stuck with him but a heap better chance of escape if they didn't. He put it to them bluntly: "You comin' or ain't you?"

They looked drop-jawed at each other. Bandle cursed.

The other digger said, "Not on your tin-type. I'm headin' for Como by the shortest route."

"Well . . . good luck," Jones told them and, picking up his rifle, struck off into the lightening gloom.

He had toyed with the notion of trying to hide out but gave this up while the sun was just beginning to outline the eastern peaks. It didn't make sense trying to hide on these flats when in mighty short minutes he would be in plain sight of any painted-face bugger who might happen to look.

He set as much store on his hair as the next; but with no place to hide a determined Injun would be likely to pass up he meant to cover what ground he could while he was able.

All he knew about the whereabouts of Bone Cabin was it had to be someplace still ahead, and the straightest line was apt to be shortest. So, scorning what fringes of brush he glimpsed, he struck out boldly, spang in the open.

This was not as foolhardy as might be imagined. With savages placing courage above everything else, in the event of capture it might make some difference in his ultimate fate, and if they figured he was crazy it could save his life.

These were some of the things rushing through his teeming mind as he watched the sun, suddenly free of the crags, come bounding across the awakening earth in a flood of golden light.

Those Shoshones, through much observation of paleface behavior, could have circled around and be watching the backtrail, setting up an ambush for their quarry to walk into. Conversely they could be miles away, larruping off with their stolen ponies, bragging and laughing in high good humor, pleased as kids with their costless coup.

Though he kept up a guise of complete indifference Jones remained sharply aware of his position. The day grew hot but he kept slogging along, step after dogged step with his throat bone dry behind cracked lips, his red-rimmed eyes haggardly alert to every lift of dust, every blur of motion. He never looked behind, never turned his head, but everything in front was subjected to thorough scrutiny. His ears ached with the strain of constant listening.

Noon came and passed in unrelieved silence. Still another hour went by without anything inimical catching at his notice. Jones began to breathe more freely, not that he figured he was safe by a long shot, but, at least, it did seem as though the bunch that had gotten away with their horses would have jumped him already if they'd had that in mind.

He did not, however, relinquish his vigilance. Those hostiles might very well have surprised Joe and Charlie in their flight toward Como and, if this were the case, only finding two men they could dang sure be on his trail right now.

His eyes burned intolerably and so did his feet in those cowpuncher boots. Every step was an agony but he kept boring on, frantically searching for some sign of that cabin.

He put a lot more stock in Mainson's surveillance than he'd thought prudent to exhibit in front of Cutteridge's daughter. He felt sure Ernest Henry wasn't writing off Como as a lost chance yet. He had watched the Philadelphian and his two college helpers board the train but there was nothing to show they had not got off someplace down the line, and there were plenty of guys for the hiring if Mainson was minded to keep tabs on Cutteridge's diggers. One or more of these could have been following Jim when he came onto that cabin. If it was *their* eyes the hunter claimed to have felt you could bet your bottom dollar that sneaky Ernest Henry would find something better to do mighty pronto than sit cooped up twiddling thumbs in some hotel room.

It was Yavapai's belief in such a possibility that had mostly pushed him into allowing Joe and Charlie to pull their freight, which he never would have done had he been fired with any intention of holding that prospect for Francie and Daddy. Chief among things he sorely wanted was some private palaver with a certain Philadelphian—and Bone Cabin, to Jones' way of thinking, held out the quickest and most likely chance.

About the middle of the afternoon, with the lavender mountains rippling and jiggling in the filmy scriggles beating up off the blistered earth, he was feverishly wondering if he ever would make it. His legs were commencing to raise charleyhorses and his feet in those boots felt like two bloody stumps. The landscape was beginning to teeter and totter and wherever he looked in that burning glare pools of water, blue and shimmering, attempted to lure him from his chosen path.

But more alarming still, when he put up a hand to brush the scrape of his cheeks not a trace of moisture showed on the back of it.

When a man quit sweating in this kind of country he wasn't far off being lunch for some buzzard.

Jones closed his eyes to fight off the panic. Then he jerked them open to go staggering on, knowing he had to get out of this sun in mighty short order or give up the ghost. You didn't have to go to Death Valley to perish. In this kind of heat, exposed without water, a man coud die just as quick on the edge of his doorstep! And them goddam mountains looked just as far off as they had this morning.

No matter how smooth they looked these flats weren't level; they only seemed that way because of the vastness of emptiness around him. They were crisscrossed by troughs and ridges and washes. And mirages, of course, at this time of day.

The place to find water was where foliage showed, a clump of mesquite, box elder or smoke brush. The trouble was sorting out which trees were real and Jones, afraid of deceit, was too far gone to risk the strength to find out. It was all he could do any more to keep putting one foot down ahead of the other.

Then, so abruptly he could scarcely believe it, topping a ridge, he saw the green blotch of trees and the bleached white walls of a cabin beneath them.

XXI

JONES, KNUCKLING his eyes, gave a kind of harsh croak when he found it still there. It could be a mirage—it looked far enough off, and those trees could be hiding a dozen red Indians. But he broke into a run, all the caution burned out of him.

He fell down twice in the treacherous sand but scrabbled to his feet again, staggering like some unjointed bird, half blinded but determined in the last gasp of consciousness to get there.

He woke in the dark, confused, unoriented, feeling like a pounded steak, his back and legs gone stiff as parfleche. He pushed his chest up off the ground, grunting with effort, and twisted his head to find himself among trees without faintest glimmer of how he had gotten there.

It was an astonishing discovery to realize that from the belt up he was wet, actually sopping—then it all came back in flashes and snatches. These must be the trees at Bone Cabin! He'd been lying in the run-off from the spring he hadn't reached. This was almost certainly all that had saved him, his abused flesh soaking up this life-giving moisture. In the state he'd been in one good drink would have finished him.

On hands and knees, lurching, head spinning, he floundered his way to the source of this trickle and, collapsing with exhaustion, put his face in the water like a horse and drank. He rolled over then, away from temptation, and lay there, listening, spent and fluttery, knowing it was surely God's own great mercy them tricky red devils hadn't found him like this.

It was this thought which, against all inclination, presently forced him to get up. He was in no position to be caught out by anyone. It was a lead pipe cinch Ernest Henry, if he came onto him, would sure as hell remember he'd some licks to get in. He might not hand a man head down above a fire but there were plenty of other uncomfortable things a guy could think up who'd been deprived of two digs plus the Lord only knew how much inconvenience.

Jones prospected around until he found his dropped rifle; it took another half hour to find his pistol. After that he sat down with his back against a wall and took stock of his situation while he masticated a chunk of the stringy jerky dug from his pocket. He got himself another drink. By that time the sky was commencing to lighten. With defense in mind he took a look at the cabin.

The thing had no windows, just a doorless hole to go in and out by, but the unchinked bone walls would offer some protection in the event of attack. Might get powerful hot but he guessed before dawn he had better move into it and, with this notion gnawing him, he scouted up a piece of dead branch and gingerly flogged the floor to discourage the presence of any hibernating snakes.

He had just straightened up to pitch out the stick when the sound of approaching horses drew him into a crouch, one hand feeling to be sure he had his pistol. This ascertained, he picked up his Winchester and put his back against a wall, ready if these were Indians coming to sell his life dearly should he happen to be discovered.

It was soon apparent the newcomers were white, but Jones held his place until scraps of conversation convinced him this was part of Mainson's outfit. Still he hung back, debating procedure until he caught the crisp tones of Ernest Henry himself. Smiling grimly, he waited to arm himself with sufficient knowledge to understand their intentions.

Mainson made this amply clear when he said, *"This* time, boys, the shoe is on the other foot. Possession, in my book, is nine-tenths of the law."

Yavapai, wolflike, stepped outside with the pistol in one hand, his rifle in the other.

It was just about light enough to pick out their gaping faces. For a couple of heartbeats nobody said anything.

Mainson had just stepped down from his saddle, was facing his horse, and the rest of his outfit—seven by Jones' count—were in various stages of unpreparedness. No one had thought to have a weapon in hand.

Yavapai grinned. "You'll git no argument from me about that. The pot's not on but git down anyways an' make yourselves comfortable. *All of you*," Jones rasped, widening his stare to take in the whole push.

He guessed it was lucky that looks couldn't kill, but one piece of carelessness was all it would take. He put one shoulder against a wall and, to let them see how little they bothered him, leaned the rifle against the bones likewise. Mainson, so far, hadn't said anything but his mouth was tighter than the fix on a well rig. It wasn't too hard to guess what the next step would be if he were given his druthers.

Beneath his sour confidences Jones felt sweat start. This crew was no run-of-the-mill bunch of diggers; more than just a couple had certainly heard the owl hoot and they weren't none of them looking to Ernest Henry for guidance. In their scrinch-eyed appraisal and misshapen features Yavapai saw all the hallmarks of barroom scrappers. He also saw that if they weren't steered off it in about ten seconds he was going to be jumped.

He said, hand tightening around the grip of his pistol, "I don't wanta have to kill nobody but the first guy down is goin' to be Mister Mainson if some of you jaspers don't git hold of yourselves."

"Hold it, boys," Mainson said after weighing him a moment. "We're not in that big a hurry."

Jones took a deep breath. "There ain't nothin' between us that can't be settled by good will an' conversation if we'll look at this thing like growed up people."

Mainson thoughtfully nodded. "You coming over to my side?"

"No," Jones said, "but with five hundred dollars and a good stout horse I'll git outa this golrammed country an' stay out."

Mainson's cheeks didn't change but suspicion stared out of his narrowing eyes. "What about Cutteridge?"

"I've had a bellyful of Cutteridge. Alls I'm wantin' is to git clean outa this."

Ernest Henry thought it over. With his still suspicious stare darkly rummaging

Jones' face he said: "Aren't you selling yourself a little short? Even as a nuisance I would pay more than that to get you out of my hair."

"Yeah." It was Jones' turn to nod. "Kind of figured you would, but I don't want no checks that can be stopped at the bank." He tried on a thin smile. "The terms of this deal is strictly cash on the barrelhead."

"You surely don't think I carry that much on me?"

"Wouldn't surprise me," Jones said. "Them's the terms. An' before you decide to pass this up you better know a couple of Cutteridge's diggers is on the way right now back to Como for help—if they haven't already got there." He let that sink in. Then he said in the tones of a reasonable man, "You been after new finds. Take a look at the bones in the walls of this shack."

Mainson, grunting, started forward. Jones stepped back to keep his gun clear and his tightening stare grimly swept the line of barroom henchmen with a warning too sharp for anyone to miss.

"All right," Mainson said, swinging around; "it's a deal. Look over those ponies and—"

"I don't need t' look 'em over. Yours'll suit me fine."

Mainson's look went blank, then a grudging appreciation of Jones' shrewdness briefly showed. "You seem to have this whole project pretty well in hand. All right, boys, break it up," he said and, then, back to Jones again, "you can put away that gun. There's only one point that bothers me." His look was intensely searching. "How do I know we can trust you?"

Jones waggled the gun. "You don't have any choice if you wanta stay healthy."

XXII

WITH THAT getaway money folded into his jeans, Jones, aboard Mainson's horse, lost no time in making far apart tracks. Trust, he remembered, was a two-way street and he didn't trust Mainson any farther than he could have heaved a bull by the tail. There wasn't anything at all to prevent the Philadelphian sending that whole crew of tough monkeys after him.

As soon as he was twenty minutes south of the parting he started looking around for a wash to drop into and when he found what he wanted, concealed from any chance of being sighted, he cut sharply left, following this dry bed of former run-offs till it bisected another angling more directly north.

This he followed for some forty-five minutes, coming into a region of rolling foothills, brushclad with thorny stubble, where he quit the sand to peer about for some way of hiding his tracks.

All this while he had ridden with the rifle racked across his lap and saw no reason for putting it up now. He paused to breathe the horse and take a quick look around. He didn't locate any sign of pursuit but appearances, he'd found through considerable experience, were something to be taken with a handful of salt.

Anxious as he was to put all possible distance between himself and that bunch at Bone Cabin he was too old a hand to run the hooves off a horse that had already been too long on the road. He permitted the animal to set its own gait while he cast about for some ground covering more durable than dirt.

He found a while later a piece of rough country angling off northeast which he thought was worth trying. A little time spent tangling up the sign could make all the difference, and he went to considerable pains to make sure anyone dogging his tracks this far would need at least one crystal ball to decipher his intentions from here on out.

With a handful of branch off this waist-high brush he worked a solid half hour before finally straightening to rest his aching back. Satisfied, now, he'd done enough to fool anyone short of an outright Injun he got back in the saddle and pointed Mainson's horse as nearly northwest as his shadow would stand for on a line calculated to bisect the N. P.'s ribbons of steel as close as might be to Medicine Bow.

It was a neat bit of figuring. They came onto the tracks two miles east of town and stayed out in the brush till well after dark, at which time he gingerly scouted the depot and, finding nobody there but a half-asleep telegrapher and one faded female with a large carpet bag, he bade goodbye to the horse and clanked his spurs inside. The key pounder reluctantly secured him a ticket after thoughtfully considering the size of Jones' proffered bribe and admitted the eastbound might be through in ten minutes. It was closer to twenty when it chuffed to a stop with a metallic screech that put a

strain on the eardrums but Jones, uncom-
plaining, swung aboard with alacrity. He
had never felt so much relief in his life. And
this feeling of well-being stayed with and
sustained him all the long way south
through innumerable stops and three delays
for changes. It was still supporting him
when, bruised and rump-sprung, three
nights later he got off the last of the spurline
coaches, tired but hopeful, back where all
his travels had started, in the smelter's glare
of booming Redskin.

He'd had plenty of time for thinking
things out and was not too frazzled about
Francie's threat to put the Pinkertons onto
him if ever he tried to slip his cable. All
laws concerning indentured servants and
bound apprentices had been a long while
lifted and what the hell else, he reckoned,
could they get him for? Any deal Francie's
daddy had made with Liz wouldn't seem to
hold water with any third party but, just to
be on the safe side, the first stop he made
was at the Sparrowhawk Bar. It didn't seem
near as big as he'd remembered.

They had a new apron behind the ma-
hogany and he put out the best bottle on
Yavapai's order. "And a clean glass, please,
while you're at it," Jones said, and peeled

a fifty dollar bill from his rubber-banded roll.

The place was packed with off-shift miners but at the sight of that roll the guy on his right, making more room for him, said under his breath, "That's a lot of long green to be flashin' in here, Jack."

Yavapai, grinning, put it away. Then he picked up his change, all but ten dollars, and told the barkeep to set them up for the crowd. In the midst of the hubbub a hand grasped his shoulder and a sardonic voice gruffly rasped in his ear, "The prodigal returneth. Or was it the bad panny?"

Jones, twisting free, found himself vis-à-vis with Fetterman. A gone-out stump of extremely black cigar poked from the side of the bouncer's gold-toothed grin. "You been runnin' with the hounds or chased by the foxes?" he wanted to know, stepping back to take in Jones' battered and trail-grimed appearance. "When Liz lent you out to that fast-talkin' dude there wasn't nothing said about returning damaged goods."

"Hoo hoo!" Yavapai sneered with the confidence of one who had his pockets stuffed with dollars. "Where's Liz? You might as well know I've come back t' pay her off."

"What'd you do—rob a bank?"

"Very funny," Jones growled, straightening up to full height and not a little put out at being lampooned by a guy who couldn't hardly write his own name. "If she wants so come out on that grubstake I lost her she better come round before I walk outa here."

Thumbs hooked into the armholes of his florid vest, Fetterman put his head on one side to say in mock terror, "Yessir, beggin' your pardon, Mister Jones. I'll be gettin' up there straightaway to tell her."

"Never mind," Jones spluttered, reddening and furious, and dug out his roll for all the world to gape at. He counted off three bills and slapped them into Fetterman's fist. "I guess these boys'll bear me out she's been paid in full fer every nickel she had comin'. An' just t' be sure, here's somethin' over fer interest!" and he put on top of it another paper hundred.

He snapped the elastic around his roll and thrust it self-righteously deep in his pocket. Leaving them gasping he spun on a heel and stalked out of the place like a wet-footed cat.

It was something to see and you can take that for gospel.

Now for the business that had fetched him back here!

He found Pop Leddabrand not in his kitchen but hunched on a stool with his back against the counter, looking as though he could count every blessing without the fingers of even one hand.

Hester's old man looked twice before he could believe and then, suddenly galvanized, jumped for the corner where he kept his sawed-off Greener. Jones grabbed the shotgun out of his hands just as the old duffer jerked the first trigger. The front window went out of its frame with a clatter. Glaring, Pop snarled, "I ort t' blast your guts all over creation!"

Jones threw the mob-queller into the street. "Chrissake, Pop! You been eatin' yer own cookin'?"

Hester's father slumped against the wall. "To think you would dast show your face in here again! Ain't you done enough to me?"

"She never come after *me!*" Jones denied, looking ringy.

"Don't you talk back t' me," Leddabrand cried. "I know what she done—an' why she did it. Playactin'!" he snarled, like it was a fate worse than death. "An' her from a re-

174

spectable, God fearing home! I can't even look my own friends in the eye!"

The old fool looked about to break into tears. "Best help I ever had, by God, an' you—"

Jones pulled out his roll, fanned the edges of the bills under Leddabrand's nose. Finding him speechless, Yavapai said, "If you figure I owe you now's the time t' speak up."

The old man gulped, put a hand out to feel them, peered again at Jones in what seemed stupefied awe. "Great Jehosophat —is them things *real?*"

"They're real enough," Jones gruffed, "an' hard come by. Here," he growled, pushing a couple of hundreds into Pop's shaking hand. "Reckon that squares us?"

"I misjudged you, boy," the old man quavered.

Jones waved away his thanks with a sniff. "Never mind that. We all make mistakes. Just tell me how I can git in touch with her."

Leddabrand, eyes popping, pawed at his whiskers. "Goddlemighty! . . . I got no idea!"

XXIII

IT WAS about on a par with catching a hoof in the gut. Jones' eyes looked about to burst from his cheeks. But even while his plans were dropping around in bits and pieces he had the presence of mind to reach out and take back his two hundred dollars.

Stomping off into the kitchen trailing language that had not been picked up from his mother he grabbed up a bottle of cooking sherry and helped himself to what relief this afforded which, by all the signs and signalsmokes, fell considerable short of any real satisfaction.

While he was hunting a dog to kick, Leddabrand, stumbling after him, cried: "I ort, by cripes, t' have the law on you—" but shrank back, blanching, at the look on Jones' face, half throwing up an arm in belated fright when Yavapai reached for him.

Jones shook the old reprobate till Pop's store teeth rattled, then pitched him against a wall down which he slid in a collapsing tangle of arms and legs. Standing over him looking like Gabriel's trumpet Jones bitterly said: "If you don't want smoke pourin' outa this place you better pull yerself together an' mighty quick think of some way fer me t' git hold of her."

He looked to be capable of burning the town down.

Leddabrand reproachfully picked himself up, gasping and shaking like a dog in a blue norther. But when Jones reached for the matches he turned off his piteous groans to cry in hurry, "Max Fittler *he'd* know! He's the one filled her head with all that— the one she run off with. Theatrical agent . . . I've got his card someplace."

"Git it," Jones growled.

The old man dug it up, Yavapai breathing down his neck till he had hold of it. "Denver!" he snarled.

"You could wire him," Pop urged, backing off to stand clear.

Jones, still scowling, stood a moment turning it over. "*You* wire him," he said. "You're her father; you'll have more weight with him than I would—an' tell him you'll have the law on him if you don't git a answer straight back that's satisfactory. Git down t' the depot an' send it *right off.*"

"All right—all right! Lemme catch my breath." A flash of cunning swiveled through Pop's stare. "Why'n't you go over to the *ho*tel an' rest? I'll fetch you the word just as quick as I get it."

Jones hesitated, peering suspiciously. "If you don't fetch it by mornin' you better be long gone."

Leddabrand scuttled for the door.

Jones filled a plate off the back of the stove, poured himself a cup of Arbuckle that smelled strong enough to float an egg.

After he'd finished this make-do supper —courtesy of the house, he grudgingly decided to take Pop's advice. He felt suddenly weary clean down to his bootsoles.

He scooped up his hat and left the place. Serve the old varmint right if somebody cleaned out the till. It was no skin off *his* nose, by godfries!

On the street he headed for the Knife & Arrow, walking perforce since he had no horse. For a camp hotel the place was not inaptly named, as most would agree after spending a night in one of its beds. They were better than cold stony ground—but not much.

Jones sighed over the cares that accompanied importance. Man with money rattling around in his pockets had a kind of obligation toward keeping up appearances; noblesse oblige and all that stuff. Perhaps because of the way he'd left Redskin he was unduly touchy. He did rather cotton to have it known he was a man who had made his mark in the world. No bindle stiff jungle for Yavapai Jones. If a suite in a hotel earmarked success he wasn't about to settle for anything less.

Clanking his spurs he stomped up its steps in fair imitation of the local cattle baron, pausing long enough to be sure he was seen in the light streaming through the yanked-open door. Then, cuffing his hat to a more jaunty angle, he crossed the cramped lobby to bang a fist on the bell, relishing the surprise he'd see on Hoffsteader's face when the proprietor came to find the cause of this racket.

But the surprise was his and plain to be seen when, bending over the register to sign, the last written line leaped from the page to stiffen him like a snout of a pistol.

Stupefied with shock he looked again but without relief. It was no hallucination. Arrogant with confidence those curlicues and squiggles, all elegant as hell, spelled *Francine Cutteridge, Canon City, Colorado.*

Jones, too panicked to dredge up a curse, got out of there fast, all but running down the fat and startled proprietor in his headlong, unseeing dash for the street. A man with a centipede up his pantsleg could hardly have shown any greater perturbation. He ran all the way to the Redskin depot, charging through its door like a locomotive, all steam and shuffing, to clutch the stationmaster in a grip of steel. "When's the next train!"

The blue coated figure blinked and goggled. "Why . . . Why it depends, I should think, on where you want to go."

Jones, eyes wild as a stallion bronc's, growled, "Never mind that—just sell me a ticket an' be sure it stops!"

"All right. You're convinced me," the stationmaster spluttered; "now let go of my arm. Next train through gets in at"—he peered at his watch—"four forty-five. That's P.M., not A.M. You'll have time to eat breakfast and—"

But Jones was already out on the platform, sprinting for the nearest livery. Inside of fifteen minutes he was on a fast horse, heading for the tules like the heelflies was after him. Matter of fact, he'd take heelfies any time in preference to Francie, he told himself, cursing.

But all things pass, and the worst of Jones' upset before long abated. If it did not unloosen all of its hooks it eased enough for him to glimpse how ridiculous a grown man looked heating his axles on account of some frail scarcely bigger than a minute. Glowering, teeth grinding, he pulled the horse to a walk, resentfully toting up the pros and cons.

Finding her booked into the Knife & Arrow had certainly given him a nasty turn. He didn't know yet how she'd got onto him so quick or why she'd figured he'd be heading for Redskin, but she had come like a bullet. That she'd got better connections was hardly surprising—another example of certain fringe benefits accruing to Daddy's wealth and influence. A plain ordinary guy couldn't hardly stand up to it.

Still . . . if he chose not to work for them, what could they do? Sic the Pinkertons onto him—wasn't that what she'd threatened? But he hadn't done anything the Pinkertons could get him for . . . had he? That deal her old man had patched up with Liz—but he'd paid Liz off and had earned every nickel he had ever got from Cutteridge. Twenty times over! he told himself, snarling.

Still muttering about it he pulled to a stop. He had dang near forgotten that wire he'd told Hester's father to send to her agent! Hell's flaming backlog! He couldn't quit town without knowing about that! What sense had there been in quitting the bone business to come back here if he was going to be stampeded out of connecting up with Hester? He had no other lead to her whereabouts?

He reluctantly turned the horse around, pointing its head in the direction of town. But with Redskin's lights buttering up the view he squeezed the horse down to a crawfish crawl while he rechecked his figuring. All systems said *Go!* but he was not reassured. Scratch a Cutteridge and you turned up a twister. There just wasn't no way of predicting that tribe, and curvacious Francie was the worst of the lot.

They might not have a goosebump to stand on but let that dame get her hooks in him again and the first thing you know he'd be back digging bones to the glory of Daddy!

There was one possible out, he thought, remembering the offer Ernest Henry had made him. Even though they'd not parted with any hugs or kissing it looked a pretty sure bet Ernest Henry would welcome him with wide open arms, agree to almost anything if it would put on his payroll the guy who'd been helping Cutteridge put him out of the running.

XXIV

WORKING FOR Mainson he could thumb his nose at Cutteridge—and it wasn't like he had nothing to trade. In his saddletramp days, and in his scouting for Miles, Jones had sure enough covered a mighty swatch of country. Cutteridge might have the edge on Ernest Henry with the longhairs and in government circles but only Jones knew where the bones were buried. And it was this kind of savvy that had put Big Daddy back onto the front pages.

He was pretty sure Mainson would let him write his own ticket, but Jones had not been called mule-headed for nothing, and proved it now by edging the hired nag back toward the depot.

He kept a hand on his pistol and both eyes skinned, keeping the horse to the blackest shadows, trying to ignore the jittery prickles that stood out like spikes all across his back. It was easy enough to say the pulchritudinous Francie couldn't do a damn thing, but persuading himself to believe this, he found, was like attempting to scratch one's head with one's elbow. He had sometimes wondered if it was Cutteridge himself or Cutteridge's daughter that kept everybody's nose to the grindstone. He'd about as soon work for Simon Legree!

Rationalization only sharpened his hackles and the more he scouted the looks of things the jumpier he got. Only a long-nourished stubbornness kept him from hopping the first train to Mainson. It was ridiculous to let a frail get under your hide—he had to keep telling himself this to stay with it.

From the covert of a patch of squatting cedars, still aboard the head-shaking horse, Jones conned the depot with a fluttery regard trying to think how he might tell if and when Fittler's answer arrived. And he reluctantly decided there was no way, short of exposing himself.

From their shaggy covert he could see the telegrapher filling his head up with lies and half-truths from a spreadopen newspaper. He didn't act like a man with messages waiting on a carrier.

Jones' impatience finally got the best of him and, tying the gelding's reins to a tree trunk—keeping as deep in the shadows as he could, he slipped over to the depot and let himself in. The ticket office was closed and there was nobody around except the man by the table with his head in the paper.

"Don't you pay no attention to the clickin' of that thing?"

"Calls my name when it wants me."

Jones let out a snort. "You got a wire fer Pop Leddabrand?"

The guy in the eyeshade looked over his paper. Yavapai didn't know him from Adam's off ox and it was mighty quick obvious the feeling was mutual. "You don't look growed up enough t' have a handle like that."

"T'ain't fer me. I'm what you might call Leddabrand's depity."

"And I'm the sheriff's uncle."

"Look, Mac." Jones said testily, "he sent me over here t' pick it up fer him."

"What's he got—a hole in the head?"

Jones tried to stay on top of his edginess. "It's about his daughter. Hester," He explained.

"Didn't reckon he had more'n the one. Been gettin' these wires from her once a week, Tuesdays, every week, reg'lar as clockwork long as I been here. Ain't never sent nobody after one yet."

Jones' eyes drew down and he pretty near swore at this all too-apparent evidence of Pop's perfidy. But, "There's allus a first time," he growled, thinking fast.

"Not at my station." This jasper was adamant. "We don't give out telegrams to every john that wants one."

Jones, uncertainly, kept on staring. He said like a guy that had been walking in his sleep, "I'm gonna make this real easy. Just a little bit ago he come here with a wire fer Denver, Colorado. To a feller name of Fiddler—"

"Not Leddabrand." The telegrapher shook his head. "He ain't been near here tonight."

"Son of a bitch!" Jones yelled like he'd been stabbed, and went tearing from the depot with his ears laid back. The telegrapher, peering after him, thought if ever he'd seen the look of murder this crazy galoot would be his first choice.

In a red fog of rage, Jones—as soon as he got himself into the saddle—pointed his surprised horse back up town and dug in the spurs. Lost clean out of his head for the moment was Francine Cutteridge and all she stood for. All he could think of right then was one thing: to grab that ornery lying old bastard and wring the God's truth out of him!

In front of Pop's place he piled out of the saddle, hit the ground running and slammed through the front door so furious mad he was shaking all over.

There wasn't a soul inside. The money drawer back of the counter was all the way out, bare as a baby's bottom. Looked like Leddabrand had put on his specs and not stayed around to wait for retribution.

Jones, ory-eyed with temper, might not have left one board upon another had he not been so prodded by the flight of time. *Every Tuesday* that key-pounder'd said. *This* was a Tuesday and *he hadn't been in there!*

With nothing to show which direction Pop had taken and no proof at all this Fiddler hadn't been born hell a-kiting of old cloth and pussywillows, Jones sent the hired horse pounding toward the depot, the cold rage inside him building up like a thundercloud. If anyone else got between him and Hester, someone, by grab, was going to pay dear for it!

He slowed the horse to a grit-throwing stop beside the railroad's yellow depot and sat a while considering before dropping his weight to the cinder-surfaced ground. Like a man in no hurry he clomped inside, put his belly against the counter and waited for the telegrapher to get around to noticing him.

"You again, eh? Well, what is it this time?"

"I'll take a squint at that wire Pop never come in fer." Jones brought his hand above the level of the counter, gave the key-pounder a look down the barrel of his pistol. "That Tuesday wire from Hester."

The telegrapher, motionless, licked at gray lips. "You're askin' for trouble, Mac."

Jones cocked his pistol.

From a wire basket at his elbow the guy took three yellow forms, shuffled through them with bulging eyes and slapped one on the counter.

Jones, picking it up, looked first for the signature then for the address and tossed it back. "I'm obliged to you, Mac. Now don't be a hero." He backed through the door, yanked the thing shut, and froze in his tracks when a harsh voice said:

"What do you think you're up to, Jones?"

XXV

BIG ASS Liz stood in front of his horse, all two hundred pounds of her, looking as crusty as the side of a mountain.

She saw the gun, all right, but chose to ignore it. "If it's in your head to take off again there's a little matter of thirty days' work—"

An outraged bleat sprang out of Jones' throat. "I've took care of that! I went to yer place soon's I got off the train a' plunked down the entire amount of that grubstake! You must think I'm a *fool!* Now git outa my way—"

"You never paid *me.*" She stood like a rock between Jones and his horse.

"I give it t' Fetterman. He's yer man, ain't he?"

She looked at him hard. "Let's see your receipt."

It was Jones' turn to stare. He squirmed, thinking back, trying to remember who'd been around them.

"You're so packed full of lies," she said, lip curled back, "a body'd think with all that practice you'd have every hole plugged." She peered at the gun he'd half raised from his side. "Put a hand on me and I'll fetch the whole camp."

Under that unflinching look Jones, reddening, put the gun away.

"Now what's it to be?" she said, smiling coldly. "You goin' to shell out an' pay up your just debts like a man or—"

"God dammit!" he snarled, "I *paid*, I told you! Why'n't you ask Fetterman—"

Her lip curled again. "He's off on vacation. As if you didn't—"

"The bar was full! Any number of guys—"

"Name me five."

"Well . . ." Jones floundered to a stop. "Hell, I wasn't payin' no attention—"

"If you think I'm goin' to question half this—"

"Oh, fer Chrissake!" Jones cried, digging out his roll. Ripping off another clutch of bills, swearing bitterly, he slammed them into her extended claw.

"Aren't you forgettin' something?" She looked up after counting. "I don't do these things for charity. Interest'll come to . . . let me see—call it another hundred even."

Jones yanked off his hat and hurled it on the ground. With his eyes like two holes

190

burnt in a blanket he peeled another century from his dwindling wad and, handing it to her was exaggerated courtesy, thrust a finger to his mouth to poke around among his molars. "By God, Liz! You missed two eye-teeth!"

Liz laughed, probably figuring she could afford to. "That's all right," she told him magnanimously. "It's that soft streak in me. I wouldn't want to kill the goose that lays such pretty eggs."

Jones caught the northbound train at Kingman.

That wire from Hester he'd made the key pounder show him had been dispatched from Denver. Probably take a deal of hunting in a place that big to track her down, but now that he was finally free of the past he was prepared to devote the whole rest of the summer to it—or for as long anyway as his money held out. His big mistake was in leaving her and he did not propose to be shook off again.

Sure she was sore. She had a right to be after the way he had treated her—he'd been dazzled, half-blinded by Francie's wiles. He'd got his eyes open now. Things was going to be different. No more boozing and helling around. It was time he reformed and, by God, he'd do it! Toe the straight and narrow if that's what was wanted to prove he meant business.

He thumbed through his roll and groaned at the inroads this excursion had cost him. But there were better days ahead. He was onto a good thing—he felt of his pocket, warmed by the thought of it; all he had to do now was to find her, explain things. She'd understand—hell, he'd crawl if he had to! There was nothing impossible to two people in love.

In the crummy stations, sitting around on hard benches, waiting on changes and schedules, impatient and fidgety, an intangible disquiet, a gray thread of doubt, began undermining his rose-colored visions.

What if she still didn't want any part of him?

It was unthinkable, of course, but the rough edge of it kept nagging, sawing away at this structure he'd projected. He couldn't honestly believe when he showed how contrite he was—how far he would go to patch things up—that she would turn him down. All they'd been to each other . . . it was all working for him. But that cold thread of doubt kept churning and twisting like the dangling shape on the end of a hangrope.

If there was any one thing he had learned about women it was not to count chickens before they were hatched.

A dismal drizzle met the train at Denver. It was unseasonably cold and the puddled streets looked as gloomy as coffins. Never a man to put off till tomorrow any business as urgent as taking care of his future, tugging down his hat, Jones set out to find her.

The first step, of course, was to locate the theaters. A chipper looking girl behind a kiosk of stogies, books and periodicals seemed like a good place to start. She smiled at him brightly. "You're not lost, are you cowboy?"

"There's a girl in this town that I have t' git hold of," Jones said, pulling off his hat politely. "She sings songs," he added helpfully. "Where you reckon I'm like t' find her?"

She picked up a book and said, thumbing through it, "Do you know if she has an agent?"

"Fittler—Max Fittler."

She turned back some pages, ran a finger down the print and frowned. "No Max Fittler here, I'm afraid." She closed the book, then opened it again on some yellow pages. "If you're sure she's here perhaps some other agent could help you." She ran her finger down the page. "Curly Ducker! He would know if *any*one would and he's just down the street, practically round the corner. The Equitable Building—you can catch a horse car. It will take you right there."

Jones thanked her and bent his steps toward a door. "Not that one—" she called; "the big door out front." He thanked her again and clanked his spurs toward it, conscious of the grins on several twisting faces.

He stood under the marquee to keep out of the rain, crowding after some others into the first car that stopped. The driver flicked his reins; the car moved off. While Jones was fumbling for change he told the driver, "I want t' git off at the Equitable Building."

"Wrong car, Jack. You want 44. I'll let you off at the next intersection."

The next intersection had no place to get under. Jones stood in the drizzle for a full half hour before the car he wanted came along. By that time, drenched and forced to hang on a strap, he was beginning to wonder if he ever would find her. The whole world seemed to be conspiring against him.

But he got off where the driver told him and stood for a moment in the rain peering around, depressed by the concrete canyon that surrounded him, looking at umbrellas, the raincoated shapes all scurrying along like a bunch of wet ants.

Gawking up at the monstrous buildings he felt suddenly dizzy, fenced in, about to smother. God—what a way to live! he thought and, remembering his mission, looked around for his destination. It was straight ahead, just cross the rain-drenched walk, less curlicued than its majestic neighbors but seven windows tall, apparently a hive of frenzied activity, people bustling in and out all the time.

Yavapai, suddenly struck with the size of this place, began to feel like he'd got into a nightmare. How did you go about finding one guy in a place big as this? He saw a door labeled STAIRS and a whole row of others with glass faces that kept sliding back and forth to gobble people or spew them out. It was enough to make a man's head swim!

Then he saw a gazebo in enough brass and braid to be at least a general in somebody's army. He had some kind of clicker in his hand that seemed to control the different sets of glass doors; every time it snapped one set banged shut, and the next time they opened a different bunch came scurrying forth—like seeds, he thought, bursting out of a squeezed orange.

Shivering in his wet britches and brush jacket Jones finally got up enough gall to accost him. "You got any idea," he said, touching his hat, "where a feller could locate a gent named Drucker?"

"Fifth floor, Jack. Room 547—right in here. Step lively now," the General said, hazing Jones through one of the sets of glass doors into a tiny closet already packed with people to bursting. The doors slammed shut; the floor pushed Jones' feet up straight through his stomach and somebody breathlessly cried out, "Three!"

The floor fell back; the doors slid open and three-four people fought their way clear before the doors with a squelching gasp slid shut.

Yavapai lost track of how often this happened but the crush kept thinning until finally, motionless, glass doors wide open on a daylighty dingy kind of hall, he found himself alone with some bloke in a purple monkey suit who stood looking him over like something had been said which Jones hadn't caught.

"End of the line, mate," this feller said.

Jones said nothing—he hadn't yet quite caught up with himself.

"You hard of hearin'?" Monkey Suit asked. Then, louder, he said, "There ain't nothin' beyond this stop but blue sky."

Jones said hoarsely, "I'm lookin' fer Curly Ducker."

"He ain't up there. Try the fifth floor, chum."

The doors slid shut. The floor dropped beneath him with a whirring rush that took Jones' breath away and filled his mouth with the taste of bile. And then, before he could tell up from down, the floor stabilized; the doors popped open and he was right back down where he'd started from, the General and himself exchanging startled glances.

Monkey Suit said, "He missed his floor." The cage filled up; the doors slid shut and the whole hurly-burly began all over. In the midst of this confusion Monkey Suit said, "Curly Ducker's floor, mate. Room 547," and Jones staggered off.

XXVI

DUCKER SAID, "Hester Leddabrand? Never heard of her."

He was a plump, oily customer with three strands of hair elaborately plastered across a skull devoid of other adornment unless one counted the bulgy eyes that crouched like skinned grapes at either side of his nose. He was garbed in store clothes that were surely the envy of the community's pimps and race-course touts, and the damply pudgy, but well-manicured fingers impatiently thumping across his desk splayed out to reshuffle themselves into a steeple.

"Look, Mac"—he slanched a glance at the clock—"you can take it from me; no canary ever come outa the sticks with that kind of monicker—not in my time. Speakin' of time, if that's all you wanted to see me about . . ."

Jones, with an effort, pulled himself together. "How about Maisee Devereaux?"

"Maisee? You know Maisee? Chrissake, why'n't you say so?" Ducker was suddenly all affability. "Now there's a real comer!" He considered Jones more closely, trying to bolster a smile that was already slipping. "Got a booking for her, have you?" His tone struggled with doubt.

"We're old friends," Jones said, and the smile came back. "You might almost say we're practically betrothed."

Ducker's jaw sagged. Not all the king's horses could make him swallow that, and he looked suddenly put upon, about two jumps from the end of his patience.

Jones said hastily, "I know how I look, but I just got in an' ain't had time t' slick up. A guy that's been two days on the steam cars—"

Ducker raised a protesting hand. "If there's nothing further—"

"Hell, I almost forgot!" Jones grinned, a little rueful. "If you could git me her address I'd sure be obliged."

Ducker stared. Jones said quickly, "I was in such a hurry t' git off from Cutteridge I—"

"Did you say *Cutteridge?*"

Jones' head nodded.

"That dinosaur feller? The one trying to prove we all come from apes?"

"I don't think," Jones laughed, "he gives a damn where we come from just so long's his name stays on the front pages."

Ducker said suspiciously, "What's *your* connection with him?"

"Well, I ain't one t' brag," Jones told him modestly, "but you're talkin' to the waddy that's been providin' him with bones, the one that's had charge of the most of his digs."

It was plain from Ducker's face he didn't know *what* to think. He said, "You're pulling my leg."

"Don't you believe it! I quit that old hypothecator over at Bone Cabin. Expect it musta just about finished him. I went all the way down t' Redskin—that's in Arizona Territory, an' what do you reckon I found when I got there? Francie Cutteridge, waitin' with both arms out."

Ducker gasped. "You never!"

"I sure as hell did—it's the gospel truth. Cross my heart," Jones threw in for good measure. "Follered me round like a dawg, she did, scairt I'd take off with some other female an' leave her ol' daddy without a leg to stand on."

Ducker's jaw hung open, plainly forgotten in the awful fascination of Yavapai's whoppers. Jones judged him about ready for the coop de grass. Leaning over the desk he skewered the agent with a glittering eye.

"You know what?" He thumped himself on the chest and laughed. "That's just what I done—left him flatter'n a last year's leaf."

Ducker sat there goggling with the hook through both gills.

"You wouldn't believe what them two has offered t' git me back—an' that's not a patch t' what Mainson's come up with. Says he'll top by three anything Cutty offers! Yessir! There's a jasper knows the value of competence!" He lowered his voice. "That's why I've got t' git hold of Maisee."

Ducker came to with a start, said gruffly: "What's she got to do with it?"

Jones looked pained. "Didn't I tell you we was just like this?" and held up two fingers tightly squeezed together. "Reason she quit me was account of Cutteridge— more likely Francie, I suspect . . . you've probably seen her pictures in the papers." Jones managed a high. " 'Fore I do any sign-in' up with Mainson I got t' see where she stands—that's reasonable, ain't it?"

Ducker passed that one. He seemed to be having some trouble sorting out what he'd been told, like he wasn't quite sure how much value should be put upon which. Shaking his head he finally said, "I can't help you."

Jones straightened up and you could see his hackles rising. "Can't or won't?"

"She's not my client. I got nothing to do with her."

"You're placin' people in her line of work. You oughta know who's showin' where or can damn quick find out."

"It wouldn't be ethical," Ducker said primly.

Chewing his lip Jones dug out his roll, slipped off a twenty and flung it down on the desk. "That help your memory?"

Ducker, looking tempted, stuck to his guns. Jones, appearing about half minded to take a poke at him, stood frowning irritably. Hard breathing he put down a second twenty, shoved the rest in his pocket and, opening his jacket put a hand on the gun that was thus disclosed.

Ducker blanched. Getting hurriedly up he waddled over to a cabinet against the far wall, yanked open a drawer, consulted a couple of cards, scrawled on a pad, tore off the sheet and handed it across like a stagecoach passenger delivering up his watch. "Just remember," he snarled, "you never got this from me!"

"Better save your breath t' pray she's there."

Outside the building, back on the street, which the rain for the moment had apparently abandoned, Jones took a look at what Ducker had written, waved up a hack, handed over the paper and heaved himself into it.

The horse's hooves rang out on the pavement, furnishing a rhythm for the whirl of Jones' thoughts. He was not at all sure he wasn't off on a goose chase; Ducker, now he thought back on it, had folded powerful sudden.

A smell of fall was in the air but it wasn't so much the time it might take on a dwindling stake to catch up with her as it was Hester herself that so sorely tormented him. What would he say to her and how would he say it? He was worried enough to be not at all sure she wouldn't slam the door on him. And it could be even worse!

There was a deepening chill way down in him someplace that sprang from a notion he didn't even want to *look* at but couldn't get away from. What, for instance, would he do if she had up and got married to one of them toughs he had seen her with at Salt Lake?

"Hell's fire, man! Has that nag gone t' sleep?" he cried, sticking his head out.

The cabby paid no attention. The horse passed some air and began to slow down, dropping into a walk and, a few strides later, stopping. "Are we there?" Jones called, half up and reaching for the door.

The driver said, "Just set back. I'll tell you when we get there."

Sounded like the rain was tuning up again. Jones impatiently bounced open the door. "This it?"

"Not yet."

"Then what the hell are we waitin' on?"

"The mare, Jack. She ain't no different from the rest of us. Every so often she just has to pee. You ever tried to pee on the run?"

Jones slammed the door. He could of made better time on a bicycle!

But after a bit they got going again and the next time they stopped the hack driver called, "Here you are, Jack. Don't see much use all that sweat an' shoutin'. Show don't start for another two hours."

Jones hadn't come to take in the show. He paid the man, searching out the exact change, then stood for several minutes looking up at the place, ignoring the fellow's affronted stare. A variety house. He scowled at the posters, not even seeing her name.

The ticket office was closed. He tried the doors, found them locked, hunched his damp shoulders and leaned against the building, not even thankful for the canopy that kept the drip away from him.

He was in too much of a swivet to stand there long. Found an alley and tramped around to the back of the place. The stage door was locked, too, and there was no one around.

He went back to the street and asked one of the passersby if there was someplace handy a man could get a feed at. "Pringle's," the fellow said, pointing. "Much obliged," Jones growled, and struck out for it.

He killed what time he could feeding his face, picked his teeth for a while, had another cup of java and went back to the theater. A man in work clothes was unlocking the ticket booth. He had a pail and a mop and a beltful of rags. "What time do you reckon Maisee Devereaux will git here?"

The guy looked around, surprised. "They've gone, mate—that whole lot. Closed last night. We got a new show today."

Jones looked like he was about to throw a fit. Then, getting hold of himself, pulled a bill from his pocket—the bill he'd have given the cabby if he hadn't been so riled. "You know where she went?"

The man peered at the bill and broke out a grin. "You're in real luck, mate. They're over at Golden—whole show booked in for a one night stand."

"Whereat's Golden an' how do I git there?"

"Hell, it ain't much more'n a whoop an' a holler. If you ain't got a rig the narrow gauge'll take you up there."

"Where's the depot?"

"Ten blocks west."

Jones shoved the bill back in his pocket and struck off.

He didn't look back, feeling somewhat on the cheap side, but who knew how much farther he might still have to go? And if he didn't get hold of Hester pretty almighty soon he would sure as hell be down to eating grass or selling out to Ernest Henry!

Of course, that wasn't strictly true but it was close enough to worry him.

XXVII

HE GOT off the train at Golden late that afternoon. The sun hung over the Front Range like a balloon getting ready to come down in a sheet of flame, and Jones, after locating the hall where her troupe was due to open, was just about ready to go up the same way. The show wouldn't start for another four hours!

If he knew where she was staying . . . but there was nobody around that could tell him. A news kid peddling on a corner caught his eye and he went hurrying over. "Son," he said, declining a paper, "you got any idea where them play actors is holed up—the ones that's puttin' on that show tonight?"

"Sure. They're all packed into Ma Flannery's—two blocks over an' one block north."

Jones gave him a dollar and struck off at a lope.

He tried to frame what he would say when he saw her, pruned up a dozen opening gambits including a remodeled grubstake pitch, and could not build any real faith on any of them. He reckoned he was going to have to play it by ear.

In an outmoded section of Golden's residential district the Widow Flannery's means of sustenance, sole relic of a husband who had gone from borrasca to an early grave, was the huge three-decker clapboard house, replete with all the architectural follies common to the homes of mining tycoons, which she had turned into a boardingplace for transient drummers and traveling actors. Had Jones been in any danger of mistaking it, the weird assortment of characters taking their ease on the broad veranda could hardly have failed to set him straight.

Striding up the path from the picket fence he took them in with a scowl which he had sense enough to hide before stopping on the steps to catch his breath. The cynosure of all eyes, he cleared his throat to say with some diffidence, "I'm looking for Maisee Devereaux. . . ."

"Maisee?" An elderly gent with a fringe of grizzled whiskers running along his jaws like a hedgerow bordering an empty field looked around the group as though for something mislaid. But one of the others, a sullen mouthed girl, with forthright malice said, "Isn't that the peroxide blonde in room four?"

"Thanks," Jones growled, and stepped through the door.

He did not have to look for the numbers because just as he came in, Hester, dressed to the nines, stepped from one of the doors along the hall, stopping abruptly to stare in surprise.

"Hes . . ." Jones said.

"What are *you* doing here?"

It was a pretty cool welcome for one who had come such a weary way. Jones, trying to swallow the fright in his throat, pulled off his hat and stood twisting it nervously.

She took in his seedy, travel-worn appearance with no sign of softening, no hint of nostalgia. "How's the bone business? I see your friend, Mr. Cutteridge, is back in the papers—"

"I didn't come here t' talk about bones."

She smiled, sugar sweet. "You surely didn't come to see *me*."

"Well, I did," Jones muttered, and took his courage in both hands. "I've been seven kinds of a parblind idjit but the only one I ever loved was you!"

Her eyes did change a little then, but not

209

much. They still showed a heavy overburden of skepticism.

"Aw, Hes," he begged, "just give me a chance. I'll make it up to you. I've got in mind a proposition—"

"I was pretty sure you had," she said tartly. "Yavapai you're a born promoter—"

"Not like you mean. You'll see!" he declared. "I'm a changed man, believe me. I've quit that high-bindin' bone huntin' crowd—"

"You can't turn back the clock," she said, shaking her head a little—sadly, he thought. "Anyway," she said briskly, "we can't talk here," and glanced toward the open door to the veranda, looking back at him searchingly. "After the show tonight, if you still feel like it, we might talk a bit. For old times' sake."

"I don't see why we can't talk now. I come all the way from Redskin t' find you—"

"That was sweet." She smiled over a shoulder. "If it's a loan you . . ."

Jones swelled up and his neck began to darken but he someway managed to grab a hold on himself. Reproachfully he said, "I come t' ask you t' marry me."

"That *is* a change." She looked him over.

"You gone back to cleaning spittoons again, have you?"

"I paid Liz off." Jones said plaintively, "Why don't you listen? I don't figger t' be a bum *all* my life! I'll be strikin' it rich—"

"Same old Slim. The man with the Mother Lode just around the corner."

Maybe he deserved it but Yavapai was getting a little tired of her needling. "Well, this time it's true," he growled, and mighty near went on to tell her about it before, with unaccustomed caution, he happened to remember the claim was still unstaked. A little resentfully he said, "I could buy this place an' pull it down if I was minded—you just wait! Better still, come back with me an' see fer yourself. . . ."

"I have to go now. Perhaps we can talk about it after the show."

They did, indeed, talk of a good many things when he walked her home from the theater that night in the light of a moon that was just made for lovers, but every time he tried to bring up the mine and his prospects of prosperity she either managed to change the subject or pooh-poohed it into oblivion.

And his every attempt to haze the talk toward matrimony got the same treatment —well, not quite the same maybe. She

211

didn't come right out and say so but she got it across that, like the most of his pronouncements, this vision of double harness was not to be taken without a deal of salt.

At Cheyenne Jones began a bit seriously to question the true worth of the adage which entreats folks with problems to "try, try again." For three weeks now he'd been in constant attendance, doggedly following the troupe from town to town, spending with her whatever time she would give him.

What with wining and dining, new clothes and travel expenses, his bankroll no longer needed rubber bands to hold it. If she was testing his endurance—the depth of his intentions, she had better be making up her mind mighty quick because, financially speaking, he'd about hit the end of his rope.

He was like that feller flanked by Charybdis and Scylla; he didn't want to let go and couldn't afford to hang on. She had thawed out considerable and, while they were not in their relationship quite back to the status enjoyed before Francie Cutteridge had snaked him out of Redskin to hunt up bones for Daddy, present indications certainly held out plenty of promise.

The night the troupe pulled into Winnemucca, Jones, dog-tired, was given a new lease on hope when Hester, at the hotel's desk, hauled him away from the others to whisper excitedly with stars in her eyes: "Slim, I'm going to be sleeping on something tonight. Keep your fingers crossed tight. I guess you did mean what you told me in Denver, about us . . . and the future. I haven't kept you dangling just out of spite; there's something about this kind of life—all the hustle and bustle, new faces and places—that gets into your blood. But tomorrow I'll have something definite to tell you." And, standing on tiptoes, she leaned toward him suddenly and gave him a kiss right smack on the mouth.

Jones, like a punch-drunk fighter, stood there wall-eyed while she sped up the stairs.

XXVIII

How LONG he stood there, locked into the gyrating whirl of his thoughts, Jones had no more idea than how long he'd been jabbered at when the voice of the old codger back of the desk finally got through to him.

"What's that?" he called, rousing.

"If you're figurin' on staying here you'd better hop at it. There's just two rooms left an' one's already spoke for."

Jones walked to the counter and wrote in the book, so obviously absentminded the old fellow whipped it gloweringly around. "Jones, is it?" he said, peering nearsightedly. "Letter here for you—been here most nigh onto a week. Room seven," he grumbled, handing down a key. After rummaging a moment, muttering to himself, he found and placed a postmarked envelope beside it. "Come in all sizes," he declared with a sniff.

Yavapai stuffed the missive into a pocket and picked up his key.

"You don't look like a drummer."

Jones, at the stairs, paused to glance back. "How's that?"

"All them add-resses. You been movin' around."

"Yeah," Jones said, and went up the stairs. Probably he thought at the edge of his mind, it was his lack of luggage that made the old fool so testy. He found Room 7, threw his hat on the bed. Tomorrow, she'd said. It was sure as hell time!

He hauled out the envelope, squinting suspiciously. It was covered with postmarks and postal endorsements. The original address, crossed out but still legible, read Yavapai Jones, care of Curly Ducker, Denver, Colorado, and had been mailed from Redskin. He didn't have to study much to know it was from Francie. Her smell was all over it.

Leaving his key in the door, the letter—unopened—still in his hand, he went back downstairs to look around for some grub. The hotel dining room was closed at this late hour but the bar was still open. He went in, ordered a beer and helped himself to a sandwich. He had another beer and dropped the letter in a cuspidor before going back to his room.

He was up bright and early, the habit of years. He took a walk, still thinking about Hester's promise and the prospect, long cherished, of getting her away from his bunch of two-bit phonies. A coyote's yammer would sound good for a change. A man belonged outside in God's open.

There was no one on the desk when he got back to the hotel and, for lack of anything better, he picked up a paper and sat down in the lobby. Cutteridge, it seemed, was working Bone Cabin now, still shipping out his petrified monsters. The only surprise in that to Jones was how he'd managed to get the place away from Ernest Henry— not that Yavapai *gave* a damn.

According to Harragan's wire-service story Daddy's latest find measured seventy feet from teeth to tail and would have weighed, it was estimated, in excess of forty tons. With a brain no larger than an ordinary orange.

Cutteridge, it appeared, had named this one *Morosaurus*, only to discover Mainson had already claimed it under the tag of *Camarasaurus*. Daddy, losing his temper, had charged Ernest Henry with predating his reports. In an adjoining paragraph Mainson made it known that if there were any monkey business the shoe was on the other foot and that, by using his influence, Cutteridge had been able to get the Mainson reports buried in some kind of red tape pigeonhole and his own pretentions published ahead of them.

Jones threw the paper aside in disgust. He wouldn't be surprised if Mainson hadn't got the truth of it. When it came to conniving, Daddy could have given Judas cards and spades.

Crossing the sun-filled lobby to see if the dining room was open for business Jones

216

was hailed by the crochety clerk who still rubbing sleep from his cantankerous gaze, got a slip from the mailrack and held it out. "Feller in 204 wants to see you."

Yavapai, surprised, looked down at the paper. All it said was *JONES*. 204.

The old grumbler, Yavapai discovered, looking up, hadn't hung around to peddle any answers. Whoever it was had probably got the wrong Jones. But just on the off chance, his curiosity whetted, Yavapai clomped his boots up the stairs. It did not occur to him to check the register or even to wonder if the fellow was yet up. He found 204 and banged on the door with customary vigor.

Nothing happened. Jones thumped again, putting more umph in it.

He heard the slap of bare feet. "Coming," someone grumbled. A bolt was slid back and Jones' jaw dropped. He goggled in sheer astonishment to find himself staring at the stockingcapped face of Ernest Henry Mainson.

The coal king's son dredged up a sour grin. "Come in, Jones—come in," he said, stepping back to hold open the door. He pulled off the ludicrous headgear, pushing a hand through his disheveled hair. "God, what a night! Don't people ever sleep in this town?"

"I slept," Jones said.

"Sit down and get the load off your feet. I suppose you're wondering what—"

"If you'd said 'how' you'd have the jackpot."

"How I found out where you were?" Mainson grimaced. "It wasn't easy. One of my contacts finally turned up a feller you had working on that dig down south of here and learned about Maisee Devereaux. I put someone to checking the western agents and he came up with Curly Ducker. Feller wasn't anxious to put me in touch with her."

"But money talks, eh?"

"It doesn't seem to have helped me a great deal with you," Mainson observed lugubriously.

Yavapai said, "How come Cutty's diggin' that Bone Cabin site?"

"I might have slipped there, but it just didn't stack up to be worth the risk. Shoshones. Pretty close to two hundred of them moved in on me. I got the notion I'd be happier in some other climate."

Mainson, cracking his knuckles, said: "Look here, Jones—you sign up with me and you can write your own ticket. Anything in reason. You can be your own boss."

"I'm my own boss now."

"For a happy man you seem pretty fiesty," Ernest Henry commented, smiling at Jones' scowl. Sobering, he said, "Guess you know what a water witch is?"

"Guy that tramps round with the crotch of a tree showin' folks where t' put holes down t' water?"

Mainson nodded. "You appear to have the gift of doing that with fossils. If you'll do it for me and keep an eye on my crews I'll pay you three hundred dollars every month of the year, throw in expenses, a secretary, bonuses, and . . ."

Jones shook his head.

Mainson stared at him, baffled. "You mind saying why?"

"I got plans of my own."

"And they're worth that much to you?"

Yavapai nodded. "I got a mine t' develop soon's I git round to it." He fished a piece of rock from his pocket, chunked it over.

Mainson studied it a moment. "Looks like float," he said, curling his lip, but Yavapai stretched out his hand with a grin. "Yep. Floats right into a million dollar stope."

Mainson, handing it back, finally sighed. "Guess that doesn't leave a whole lot to trade with. You've got a good thing there if you know where the—"

Yavapai chuckled. "You better believe I do."

But downstairs again, waiting on Hester, remembering that Mainson had no more scruples than a wounded cougar, he did get to worrying some. The claim was wide open; he hadn't filed on it yet and Ernest Henry or anyone else who happened to stumble onto that ledge could preempt his rights and leave him without even part of a leg to stand on.

Impatience rode him like a fever and, after cooling his heels for another half hour, he went into the dining room and ordered his breakfast. It might as well have been sawdust for all the taste or pleasure he got out of it.

He was just pushing back to roll himself a smoke when Hester came in with a couple of the other gabby frails in her outfit. Jones got up but she waved him back. "I can't talk now." She tossed him a smile. "I'll see you this noon." And off she went to find a place with the others at a table across the room.

Jones smoked and glowered. It hadn't been like that with her in the old days. Before he'd gone off with Daddy and Francie she would no more have thought of putting him off than she would of patting a white-striped skunk!

He'd been too damn easy—that's what it was. Tagging her around like a fuzzy-faced dog!

He ground out the butt of his smoke in his plate, dropped some change on the table and left the hotel, feeling hard used and pretty raunchy about it.

Still worried and graveled he turned into a pool hall. Smacking gutta-percha balls across felt did not noticeably improve either his outlook or patience. He quit the place to look around for a barroom, finally found one open and spent the hours bordering on nursing his bile with jolts of Old Crow.

Give a woman a inch she took a mile every time!

More he considered all the thought and long green he had lavished on Project Hester—his own phrase for this was "bringin' her to her senses"—the more resentfully furious his mood became. Serve her right if he took old Ernest Henry up on that offer!

Full of gusty oaths and Golden mixed

drinks he sashayed forth to relocate the hotel. Hi gollies, he'd look Mainson up and show Maisee Devereaux who wore the pants!

In some crazy way this was a satisfying thought; but, like most satisfactions, doomed to flower and fade between two blinks of the eye.

The first person he beheld upon turning into the lobby was old Pop Leddabrand, feet upon a sofa, reared back beneath a derby with a cigar stuck in his face.

Jones advanced belligerently but, just as he was about to show and tell, Hester herself stepped around a post and snuggled his arm with a pleased little purr. "So there you are! I've been looking all over. I don't know about you," she laughed, sweeping him along, "but after all that rehearsing I'm just about ready to eat one of those bones you dug up for Cutteridge."

Jones would have said something about her old man popping out of the blue had he got half a chance, but she found them a table against the far wall and a waitress came up and, after she went away with their order, Hester said, looking up at him from under her lashes, "I guess you know Henry Mainson is here?"

Yavapai grunted. He was reminded right then of that drinking he'd done, hoping she wouldn't notice. He guessed he ought have chewed up some cloves.

"He thinks pretty highly of you," she said, watching him. "He told me about that splendid offer he made."

Jones grunted again.

"That was really very handsome. Mr. Mainson's a real gentleman. So polite, such lovely manners. If you like that kind of work—"

"I didn't come here," Jones growled, "t' talk about him. I don't need his dang job."

"You're not going back to prospecting, I hope."

Yavapai stared, eyes narrowing. "So he brought that up, too!"

"Are you going to be content to waste your life chasing rainbows? How old are you, Slim?"

"Thirty-four," Jones said, scowling.

"If you're going to get ahead in this world now's the time. Why don't you be sensible? Accept Mainson's offer and I'll marry you tomorrow."

Jones looked at her. "An' if I don't?" he said, beligerent.

"I want a home," she said, "and a husband I can be proud of."

Jones, rearing back with his cheeks twisting, darkening, came within half a breath of cutting his nose off to spite his face. All those months of loneliness, of wanting her, came within an ace of being wiped out by spleen. He had his mouth wide open, about to advise her not to wait on him, when a vision of life without her—of growing old and helpless with no one around to fetch and carry—let a good deal of the wind from his sails.

He backed off to chew his lip with the eyes rolling around in his head like marbles but finally, shutting his mouth, he was able, bearing down on it, to jerk his head forward and back a couple times.

"I'm tired of—"

"Sure. I know you are," he grumbled, "an', believe me, things is goin' t' be different. But I don't have t' work fer Mainson t' prove it. Take a squint at this!" and he pushed over the chunk he had shown Ernest Henry.

She had been around mining camps long enough to know jewelry rock when she saw it. Eyes open wide she stared at Jones, startled. "Why, its *gold*," she exclaimed, and peered at it, breathless.

"You're dang tootin'!" Yavapai chortled. "An' plenty more of the same all tucked away snug just waitin' fer Yours Truly to come an' dig it outa the ground!"

She was like a different person, eyes staring down at it, big around as saucepans, cheeks flushed and breathless. Jones let out a great belly laugh, all his anger forgotten. "You stick with me, kiddo, and you'll be wearin' diamonds an' pearls. You'll make the President's wife look like a stuffed owl."

"Oh, Slim!" she cried with her voice all trembly.

"You been wantin' a home, I'll build you a castle." Jones grinned and, digging again into a pocket, opened a work gnarled hand to shove across the table a tiny vellum covered box. "Denver's best—go on, open it."

All the phonies, he noticed, were craning their heads. Let 'em look, he thought, chuckling. Let 'em get a real eyeful! It was for this kind of moment he'd been eating his heart out all the long weeks he'd spent stomping around after her.

Her fingers, fumbling with the box, at last got it open. Cheeks drained of color she just sat there, speechless, staring and staring like she couldn't believe it.

"I—I must be dreaming," she quavered.

"Not a bit of it," Slim told her. "Didn't I just tell you you'd have diamonds?" And, leaning over the table with the others crowding around, he slipped the ring on her finger. And she kissed him, hanging on like she never would let go.

XXIX

JONES DIDN'T care if all of Golden stood watching. It was a far cry for sure from the days when he had been cleaning gaboons for Big Ass Liz at the Sparrowhawk Bar. And he had earned every bit of it!

"When is the wedding coming off?" someone asked and Jones, breaking loose, turned to find Ernest Henry genially standing by their table.

"Oh, Mr. Mainson! Isn't it wonderful?" Hester asked, showing him her ring.

Agreeing that it was, he declared it was hard to tell which shone brightest, Yavapai's diamond or Hester's eyes. "I expect," he smiled, "congratulations are in order, and if you tie the knot today I might even be prevailed upon to be best man."

Hester hugged him, too, but she said that wouldn't be possible. Her contract stipulated two weeks' notice and she was a girl who truly believed in living right up to the letter of things.

Mainson, commending her, avowed that while such principles must certainly command the respect of all there was surely no reason why she shouldn't do both. They smiled at each other and while she was considering the merits of this proposal a younger edition of the establishment's night clerk stuck his face in the door to call: "Mister Jones? Mister Jones? Telegram for Mister Jones!"

Every head twisted. Several mouths popped open. No one but persons of unquestioned importance had even in Golden got a telegram before. Jones, a bit flushed with so much attention, put up a hand. "I'll take it here, garsone," he said like a prince.

The caller disappeared and shortly returned with a bit of folded yellow paper. "Shall I put it on your bill, sir?"

"Keep your pants on till I look at it."

Spreading open the paper Yavapai stared,

noticeably paler, while a warmer color crept cheekward from his collar.

"What is it?" Hester said, and moved to look around his shoulder.

Jones, scowling, read it through once more and Maisee Devereaux said in the tone of a curse, "That woman again!" and peered at him fiercely while the rest of them stared and Mainson with raised eyebrows found his interest divided—though not impartially—between the two of them.

Jones, catching his questioning glance, said uncomfortably, "Them Shooshonnies've got Cutteridge."

They stared at each other. Mainson said hopefully, "They've killed him?"

"I dunno. She wants me to come up there an' git him away from them."

Yavapai's eyes, widening suddenly, went clean away and he whacked his thigh with a wolfish grin.

Hester said, stiff and bony with concern: "You're surely not going!" She caught his arm. "It's a trick—can't you see?" She appealed to Mainson. "She's heard about us and she's trying—'

"I don't know," Mainson said. "You're probably right. That Cutteridge outfit would stoop to just about anything, but theres an awful lot of Indians camped round that dig and they were pretty well worked up when I left."

"I don't know," Jones said, "if I could live with myself, leaving a white man in the hands of them savages without lifting a finger. It ain't rightly human."

Hester let go of him as though she'd found herself holding a snake. Mainson picked up the telegram. "She's expecting a reply."

Jones said, "Yeah," with that faraway look still leaching through the glance he put on the clerk. "Can you see that a message gets sent straightaway?"

The clerk said he could and handed Jones a pencil. Yavapai licked it and on the back of the menu laboriously wrote: *WILL COME IF YOU GARANTEE RELINQUISHMENT ALL CLAIMS TO DIG I OPENED SOUTH AND EAST OF GARDEN PARK.*

Mainson, reading it across his shoulder, said, "So that's where the gold is. That's why you haven't filed."

Jones, twisting his head, showed a threatening grin to the paleontologist. "Don't *you* start workin' up no ideas. If that claim gits jumped I'll know who t' shoot."

Never looking at Hester he gave the clerk the message and the man hurried off. Mainson wandered off, too, and found himself a place at a table nearer the door. The boss of the troupe gathered up his players, paused to mutter a few words at Hester, and hazed them off through the lobby toward another rehearsal. Hester fingered her bag. "Looks like I'm going to have to eat and run."

Yavapai, grunting, dug into his food, knowing she was watching him, adopting a scowl as his best defense. It didn't stop her from saying, "The whole thing's a trick. She just wants to—"

"I can't help what she wants," Jones grumbled. "If I wanted *her* I wouldn't come huntin' you—that oughta be plain enough."

She just picked at her plate; she was too upset to eat. "I should think by this time you could see what she is. Vain, spoiled and selfish as they come! She thinks all she has to do is snap her fingers and any man will—"

"I'm not blind," Jones growled. "I know what she is, but you're missin' the point. Mainson saw it right off. That ledge is on ground her ol' man's got a lease to."

"The Colorado law—"

"Ho hoo!" he jeered. "The law never got in Cutty's way that *I*'ve noticed. He's got enough friends in important places to steal Mr. Grant's golrammed eyeteeth if he wanted 'em! It's the reason I ain't already filed on that claim. I don't want no trouble—"

"Then for the love of Pete use your head for a change! It's not your fault he's in bad with those Indians. Stay away from him!" she cried like she was just about ready to burst into tears.

And she was right to look on the dark side of this because even a kid in three-cornered pants might have guessed from Jones' jaw he wasn't about to let no mine get away from him. He kept on with his chewing, bristly as a one-eyed porcupine with chilblains. He said through his eating, "If it's any kind of a trick she won't answer."

But Hester with that girl on her mind was like an old mule with the bit in his teeth. Impervious to reason, seeing only her fears, she played her trump card. "If you leave me now, you needn't bother to come back!"

XXX

JONES, BLACKLY scowling, kept on with his eating. With the room emptied now—except for themselves and a curious waitress surreptitiously ogling them from afar—the silence piled up and grew bleak as stone walls behind two churning minds that were filled with resentment.

Hester, staring down into her lap, kept twisting the ring around on her finger. Jones, finished, pushing back, began to twist up a smoke and was still bitterly puffing—a stack of butts in his plate—when the fellow he'd given his message to send came back with another bit of folded paper.

Jones opened and read it, tossed the sheet to Hester. There were only four words: *TERMS SATISFACTORY PLEASE HURRY.*

"So you're going," she said, like the words had been wrenched from her, and eyed him unreadably.

Jones grimaced. There were a whole heap of things he was minded to say but found no encouragement in that hazel stare. He shrugged and got up.

"Here—you'd better take this," she said, cold as a well chain, and screwing the ring off, tucked it back in its box and pushed the box toward him.

Jones, chewing his cheek, picked it up and walked out. He paid his bill at the desk and hustled down to the depot. There was a train he could get in about twenty minutes that would put him into Como around noon tomorrow; but when he reached in his pocket all his fingers came out with was a five-spot, three ones and a couple of silver dollars.

Glaring, he said, "I'll be right back," and took off for the street like the heelflies was after him.

He went into a place that had three balls over the door, showed the guy Hester's ring and came out with thirty dollars. The train was already in and tooting for departure. By not bothering with a ticket, but running all out, he managed out of breath to scramble aboard the last car.

"I just hope you're not too late," Francie cried.

She looked as if she had not slept for two

weeks. Her eyes were red and puffy and she was there to grab his arm when he stepped from the train.

"How long has he been gone?"

"Since the night before last—it was over at Bone Cabin."

"You better start at the beginning. You got any idea where your father is now?"

"That's the first thing Major Updyke asked—but how *could* I?"

It was a Saturday night, she reminded him, and the whole push—except for the cook, Cutteridge and herself—had gone off to town to blow in their wages. Just short of dark six half-naked Indians had ridden into camp, knocked the cook loose of his cleaver, tied Daddy on a horse, and taken off hellbent in a cloud of dust.

"And left you behind?" Jones stared at her, astonished. "Never even—"

"I told you," she snapped, chin up, cheeks aflame. "The only one they looked at twice was Daddy. One of them, pointing at him, said: 'You come!' When he started to protest two others caught hold of him, tied his hands and put him on a horse." She said wildly, "I grabbed up the cleaver. Something hit me. Time I got to my feet they were gone—Daddy with them!"

In Yavapai's experience this simply didn't make sense.

It was hard to believe six able-bodied savages would leave a dish like Francie unraped, unharmed, free to wag her jaw. He shook his head, baffled. "You must at least have seen which direction they took."

"They went off toward the mountains."

"You sure they wasn't Seminoles?"

She said, half angry, *"Indians,* I told you. They all look alike!" She told hold of his arm again. "Don't just stand there—do something!"

"This major," Jones said. "Where'd you see him?"

"He was with the lieutenant."

"What lieutenant?"

"The one with the patrol."

Jones, grimacing, freed himself. "If it ain't askin' too much you better tell me again. This time tell all of it."

"I told you all of it—why don't you *listen?"*

Jones took a deep breath. "All right. Them redskins rode off with your ol man. Then what happened?"

"I was frantic," she said.

Yavapai nodded. If it kept on like this he'd get a string of spools and join her. He scrubbed a hand across his cheeks. "So when this major come by the next mornin'—"

"It wasn't the next morning. They came by the same night."

"That's news," Jones said. "How many horse soldiers was in this patrol?"

She looked a bit vague. "Fifteen, a dozen—what difference does it make?"

"I'm tryin' t' git the picture. How long after the Injuns took off would you say it was?"

"An hour—two hours. I didn't look at a clock!"

"All right. You told the patrol they headed off toward the mountains. What did the patrol do then?"

"They went after them."

Jones scrinched his face up. "They been back since?"

Francie shook her head. "If all you're going to do is ask questions," she said bristling, catching hold of him again, "you might as well—"

"All right. Don't cripple me. I'm goin'," Jones growled, "but first I want that agreement. In writin'. With yer name signed to it in some way that'll bind your father—"

"Don't you trust us?"

"Let's not git in no discussion about that." He pointed her toward Finter's telegraph cubbyhole.

The key-pounder said, "Hi! Long time no see."

"Yeah," Jones said. "Give Miss Francie here a paper an' somethin' t' write with." When the materials were provided he told Daddy's daughter, "Just write what I tell you. Ready?"

She didn't much like it but she finally picked the pen up.

"To who it may concern. I, Francine Cutteridge, do hereby on behalf of self and father—the celebrated professor who formerly employed him to find and excavate fossils—do hereby give, relinquish and waive all claims both now and in future to any and all Colorado digs with which we've been connected to our good friend and colleague Yavapai Jones. I do this of my own free will in exchange for services rendered."

When she stopped writing Jones looked it over. "Sign it."

Her look would have withered a white oak post but she put her name to it and threw down the pen. "You got a notary seal?" Jones said, to Finter and, when the man nodded, Jones said, "I want it on there."

When they got outside Francie said: "I'm going with you."

"That wasn't part of the deal."

She glared at him, furious. When his face didn't change she cried, in a temper, "You're the damdest man I ever ran into!"

"Feelin's mutual."

She gasped, got hold of herself and switched to cajolery. "I won't get in the way—honestly. Why, I'd go nuts waiting here with nothing . . ."

"If you fetched a spare horse you could trot along home. But if you just brought the one," Jones said, "I'm goin' t' need it an' I don't want him foundered tryin' t' pack double."

She hadn't thought to bring two. The one she had come on was back of the shack. Jones let the stirrups out, yanked up the cinch, Francie watching sullenly.

Swinging up, Jones said, "You might keep in practice by makin' eyes at Finter," and while she was digging from the tatters of that he told her soberly: "First chance you get you better locate a horse an' hit out fer Bone Cabin. Case that patrol got real lucky an' found him."

He was twenty yards off, holding the

pony to a walk, when she let out a shout. "You fool! You're going the wrong way!"

Jones didn't even turn his head.

He might be going the wrong way but reckoned his guess to be as educated as anything curvaceous Francie could dredge up. He was *not* going to make the same mistake as that cavalry and go tagging after heap of plain-to-read horse tracks that, when you needed them most, was going to split off into forty directions!

Based on their actions as reported by Francie—who ought to have, anyway, got straight what she had seen—he was prepared to take a calculated risk, bolstered by the thought that if the peppery professor was still among the quick another few hours squandered in discovering him wasn't like to make any great amount of difference.

He struck out for the river.

According to their lights that cavalry detail was taking the only course possible. He didn't know the officers but seventy percent of commissioned personnel dispatched for tours of duty at these isolated posts didn't know much more about redskins than Francie. Either punishment or politics was generally responsible for getting officers relegated to the western frontier. It was a hell of a system but the East never did take the West very seriously.

He reckoned he could be plumb wrong on this but, to a man of Jones' experience, the facts of this deal as related by Francie appeared so unlikely only one conclusion seemed possible. The man who dealt with feathered heathens and went off half cocked was pointing himself toward a mighty short hereafter.

Jones proceeded to make haste slowly with both eyes wide open and with no intention of running the heels off his pony. If he'd guessed wrong about this nothing but some powerful quick maneuvering in the pinch was going to keep his hide intact.

He didn't take the best going but stayed as much as he could to the cover of brush wherever there was any. When he came to the river he stopped to study the terrain in all directions before crossing to follow the stream cautiously west.

This was not the direction those buggers had taken but it was nearer, he figured, to where they'd wind up at—allowing for Indian whims not predictable. "You come!" they'd told Cutteridge and that, to Jones' thinking, paved the way for the rest.

From Como he'd gone north to intersect

the river and now, following it west, he drew the rifle from its boot and rode with heightened care. If he rode far enough, this present course would take him to the Seminole Reservation but, unless he'd guessed wrong, it wasn't at all likely he'd find the ones he was looking for there. Some of these Injuns had a hell's smear of pride, and if a chief, by any chance, was back of this caper he'd be wanting a place more fitting to his dignity.

The hole-up could be anywhere and Jones, not wanting to botch this, pulled his horse down to an even slower pace. No signalsmokes were going to herald the location.

He thought of Hester with regret but there'd been nothing else he could do. If it had been just Cutteridge he wouldn't have lifted a finger, but when Francie's telegram had put this deal up to him the chance to sew up the source of that gold had been too inviting for a man to let slip.

He squirmed at the remembered look of Hester's face when she'd pulled off that ring, slammed it back in its box and told him to take it; but at least he could stake his claim now with confidence, and gold was something a feller could count on.

He caught the mumble of voice sounds

before he saw them. And the first thing seen clearly after worming through the brush were the tops of several tepees. He didn't see any smoke but he could smell the fire.

With a healthy care he tied his horse in the brush, left his spurs on the saddle and gingerly edged toward the tang of burning wood.

It was always smart with Injuns to avoid any chances that weren't forced on you. He had learned the hard way that red men and white held divergent views on just about everything, but he was frequently inclined to think the Injuns made more sense. They might harangue half a night, piling boast on boast till you felt like puking, but when it came to killing enemies they didn't pass out hugs and kisses before getting ready to drive in the steel.

They was orating now.

Swinging their jaws and roasting meat.

He eased back to his horse and climbed into the saddle. Still holding the rifle he bade goodbye to caution and kneed the animal out of the brush, riding openly towards the gathered assemblage past the pole and hide shelters with as much aplomb as though he'd received an engraved invitation.

When he was sure of being seen he slid the rifle back into its boot and, still advancing, held up a hand. He knew enough about Seminoles to know he'd guessed right.

They were all sitting around the fire in a circle, chewing fatted pony and living it up like a pack of wild hogs, Cutteridge ensconced as obvious guest of honor.

Grinning sourly Jones called out his greetings. They were sure as hell doing old Daddy up proud.

Some, after being put to all this bother, might have shown a few scowls. Not Yavapai Jones. After listening to Francie's account he'd suspected he might walk into something like this.

Cutteridge waved a negligent hand. "Thunderhorse hunter—used to work for me," he said to the chief as though parading a prodigy.

Jones waved back, no longer gnawed by twinges of conscience. Minding his manners he stepped over to the chief and with appropriate jargon gave the old man Francie's brand-new repeater, helped himself to some meat and, hunkered down, began to chew horse like it was something he'd looked forward to.

He didn't tell her father Francie was worried; it didn't seem the time to be handing out reproaches. The sun rolled closer to the western mountains. Speech followed speech after the manner of powwows in the last shank stages without any put-ins from Thunderhorse Hunter.

When the shadows began pretty definitely to lean and Jones reckoned he had stayed long enough for politeness, he belched, stretched and got to his feet. "Expect," he said, shaking hands with the chief, "I better mosey along."

"If you happen to see her, you tell Francie," Cutteridge said, "I'll be at Bone Cabin maybe Monday a week. Chief's pretty pleased about my efforts in Washington. Got a place he wants to show me that he calls 'Many Thunders'—some boneyard, apparently, you must have overlooked." He swelled his chest with importance. "I belong to the tribe now, been made a blood brother."

He looked Yavapai over from the height of this accomplishment. "It's like I've always said," he declaimed. "You treat Indians right, they'll treat you the same way. Harragan ought to get a picture of this."

"If I happen t' bump into him I'll mention it," Jones said. He got onto his horse, waved again, and rode off, wondering if he would still find Hester in Golden after he got through staking that claim.